RESCUING ANNABETH (SPECIAL FORCES: OPERATION ALPHA)

TEAM CERBERUS BOOK 3

MELISSA KAY CLARKE

Dedication

For every person who has walked this dream with me,
giving me encouragement, strength and support.

My God,
My family,
My friends.

I am grateful.

This book is a work of fiction. Names, characters, places, and incidents are products of the author's imagination or used fictitiously. Any resemblance to actual events or locales or persons living or dead is entirely coincidental.

Cover by Eva Talia Designs

Dear Readers,

Welcome to the Special Forces: Operation Alpha Fan-Fiction world!

If you are new to this amazing world, in a nutshell the author wrote a story using one or more of my characters in it. Sometimes that character has a major role in the story, and other times they are only mentioned briefly. This is perfectly legal and allowable because they are going through Aces Press to publish the story.

This book is entirely the work of the author who wrote it. While I might have assisted with brainstorming and other ideas about which of my characters to use, I didn't have any part in the process or writing or editing the story.

I'm proud and excited that so many authors loved my characters enough that they wanted to write them into their own story. Thank you for supporting them, and me!

READ ON!

Xoxo

Susan Stoker

ACKNOWLEDGMENTS

A few years ago, I stumbled across the novel, *Protecting Caroline* by Susan Stoker and like many others, fell in love with the story and the characters. Being an aspiring author, I thought I would love to one day write a gripping story like that - love, romance, intrigue, suspense with a beautiful leading lady as strong as Ice (pun intended) and a hot, alpha male.

In 2017, I discovered Susan had a Kindle World and she allowed me to write in it. I was new to the process, but she gave me advice and encouragement. I blew up her messenger box more times than I probably should have but not once did she get angry or frustrated. As a result, *Protecting Joselyn* was a success - more of one than I ever dreamed possible.

So, here I am back again - a lot less messages, a whole lot wiser and still just as grateful. Thank you, Susan, for all your advice and help but also thank you for lending me Wolf and the others to help my guy get his lady back.

CHAPTER 1

The plan had been checked, double checked and checked again. Every contingency had been calculated, examined and then improved upon until everything was airtight. With a nod, the man gave his approval, and the countdown began.

30 days

Today was one of the worst days ever.

Annabeth didn't know what she had done to piss off the karma gods, but here she was, living the dream. Maybe they felt she had been a little too lucky in life lately, or perhaps they just didn't like gingers today, but either way, it was obvious she was having an extremely crappy day.

She glanced down at the broken key in her hand

and then to the other half barely peeking out of the lock in her door. What else will go wrong? Staring at the window pane, she contemplated just breaking the glass to get into her condo but discarded the idea immediately. With her luck, she wouldn't be able to get it fixed quickly, and she'd come home to a cleaned-out house. Annabeth didn't live in the worse part of Atlanta, but it wasn't the best either, and she was very attached to her possessions.

"Annabeth?"

Annabeth whirled around and pressed her hand against her chest, panting heavily. "Lord sake, Ms. Clara, you about gave me a heart attack."

Seventy-something resident cat lady, Clara Fisher stared at her neighbor. "Are you alright dear?" She glanced at the front of Annabeth's clothing. "Dear heavens, what in the world happened to you? It looks like you got into a fight with Smokey, the Bear and lost."

A dark gray ball of fluff affectionately named Precious mewed her welcome as she wove around Annabeth's feet. Reaching down, she let her fingers run over the smooth fur. Gollum sat behind his mistress cleaning his white and black mottled fur, and Samwise watched from the cracked door beside him. It still tickled Annabeth that her elderly neighbor loved the J.R.R. Tolkien classics. They often had discussions centered on the books. However, even their mutually favored subject was not enough to temper her mood. Looking down, Annabeth barely kept the overwhelming desire to throw something in check. Black burn holes dotted the front of the Kelly green two-piece suit, and a huge brown wet stain decorated the entire outfit. Her favorite go-to outfit was ruined. She stood and faced her neighbor. "Yes'm," she sighed heavily. "I'm having a little bit of bad luck today." The words tumbled out of her mouth in one long diatribe.

"I woke up late because my alarm didn't go off on time, so I had to hurry to get ready. I had an appointment with a potential new client this morning, and since I was going to be late, I called her and let her know. Considering the name of her book is *Taking Control of the Uncontrollable*, she wasn't happy, but was still willing to meet with me. The traffic was bumper to bumper on the interstate, and the vehicles were going seventy-five miles an hour, which scares me half to death. After all this time driving in Atlanta, you'd think I'd be used to it, but it still bothers me. You know you can't slow down, or they will run slap over you. So, to get my nerves under control and because it's a beautiful day, I had the roof down. Next thing I know, some Bozo in front of me throws a cigarette butt out his window, and it lands in my lap. Sparks went everywhere. I looked like one of those huge sparklers you get on the fourth of July. I was slapping at myself, trying to put myself out, swerving all over the place. It's a wonder I didn't wreck and kill myself right then and there! I guess this suit or the chemicals the dry cleaners use was flammable because, I caught on fire, big as you please. Only thing I had to put it out with is a half-full cup of coffee from yesterday that was still sitting in the cup holder. By the time I got the fire out and drove onto the shoulder of the road, an officer came up behind me. He'd seen me swerving all over the road like I was high on Aunt Helen's spiked apple cider on New Year's Day. I told him what happened, but I guess he was having a bad day also because he didn't even flinch. Instead of having sympathy for me, he gave me a ticket for reckless driving. After he left, I decided to call my client to reschedule, only to realize I couldn't find my phone." Annabeth laid her head back against the wall and slowly banged it. "It took me ten minutes to find my cell wedged between the seats and call her but by then she had decided I wasn't a good fit and is going to another agent. I finally got home and broke the key off in my door.

With the way my day has gone, it's a wonder I'm not in a ditch with my throat cut by a flying sandwich wrapper."

"Lord a mercy! Did you tick off one of them voodoo people the last time you were in Nawlins?"

Annabeth shook her head. "I don't think so. I try my best always to be nice to people. My mama would skin me six ways to Sunday if I were ever rude to anyone."

"Your mama raised you right." Ms. Clara patted Annabeth's arm soothingly. "Call the management company. They'll send someone over lickity-split to fix that lock for you. I have a feeling the day is going to be much better very soon."

"Gosh, I hope so." Gratitude swept through Annabeth as she pushed away from her door. "Thank you, Ms. Clara, I apprec..." the last of the word disappeared as she lurched forward, her foot caught under the cute entry rug lying on the floor. It had been a gag gift from friend and client, Joselyn Chambers last Christmas. On it was a picture of Lionel Richie with *"Hello, is it me you're looking for?"* written underneath. It still cracked her up every time she saw it. However, today it seemed to grab her by the shoe and throw her down on the floor. Twisting to keep from taking out Ms. Clara with her, she landed hard on her knees and face-planted in the hallway.

"My gracious! Annabeth are you hurt?"

Rolling over to sit, she surveyed the damage. Both knees had carpet burns, and her wrist ached. Moving it slowly, she shook her head. "It doesn't look like anything is broken except maybe my pride." Raising her hand, she rubbed her chin and checked her fingers. She had a scrape that was bleeding. Letting out a sigh, she drew her feet up and then let out a cry of dismay. "And my Miu Miu heels. Dang it!" She leaned over, grabbed the two-inch wedge in her fingers and looked at it forlornly. "They were still new. I got them the last time I was in California. I've never had designer shoes before."

Ms. Clara studied Annabeth a moment as she sat on the floor and fingered the remains of her $700 shoes. "Don't move from that spot. I think it's safer for everyone. I'll call the management company for you and light a fire under them to get on over here now." She disappeared into her apartment. Annabeth heard what sounded like whispering.

"Are you alright in there, Ms. Clara?" she called out.

"Oh, I'm fine, dear," she answered and appeared with a cordless house phone in her hand. "I have it set up as speed dial number three on my telephone, right after my worthless son, James, and my lawyer who's also named James and equally worthless. While I'm taking care of this, you call that handsome young man that's been making you smile this last year. The one with all the muscles and the twinkle in his eye that makes me remember my sweet Henry, God rest his soul. Lord, I miss that man. He got us thrown out of a drive-in movie once. I don't expect you remember what those are? Drive-in movies? Henry loved to take me there, especially after James was old enough not to go along if you get my meaning?" She wiggled her white eyebrows suggestively.

Annabeth didn't want to think about what trouble the older woman had done to warrant eviction from a movie. Instead, she listened as Clara contacted the company who promised to send someone over immediately.

"Now, that's done." Ms. Clara placed the headset on the table next to the door. "It's your turn. Go on and call your honey. I promise you; it'll make you feel better." Ms. Clara picked up Annabeth's cell phone from where it had landed when Annabeth fell and held it out.

Annabeth looked at her phone and shook her head. "Hick's just a good friend." Yeah, a good friend

- one with an intimate twist. They were dating but in a completely casual manner. At thirty-three, Annabeth knew she was just this side of being a cougar by seeing twenty-eight-year-old Levi "Hick" Salter. Quite honestly, she wasn't sure what he saw in her. He was a sculpted Adonis with dirty blonde hair, caramel brown eyes, a square jaw and the cutest dimples you ever saw. Of course, his nose was a bit too wide and his brow a tad too heavy to make him model perfect, but that was alright with her. He was still hotter than an Atlanta sidewalk in August. Not to mention, he was fit, which was only right for a badass Navy SEAL. She, on the other hand, was at least fifty pounds past what was socially acceptable, red hair that looked almost orange in the sun, green eyes and a fair complexion dotted with freckles, all courtesy of her Irish grandmother's genes. She had learned a long time ago to love herself and turn a blind eye to those who would make her feel inadequate. Being with Hick did more to booster her self-worth than anything else.

Ms. Clara pushed the telephone into Annabeth's hands. With a grin, she tapped the surface with one gnarled finger. "Go ahead and call him. Leave a message. Everything will be much better afterward. Lord knows just hearing that young stud talk gets my knickers in a twist. He has that deep voice that has all kinds of promises and none of them safe for church. If I were fifty years younger, I'd find me one of those boy toys just like him. The excitement would probably do me right in, but it'd take the mortician a week to pry the smile off my face."

"Ms. Clara!" Shock froze Annabeth's fingers to the cell.

Her neighbor laughed and leaned in whispering conspiratorially. "As they say, snow on the roof but a fire in the furnace. Now go on, call him. You won't regret it."

Her fingers ran over the smooth surface several times. The screen flashed to life, and Annabeth saw one of their puzzles. It was their thing - they sent each other emojis that represented a well-known book or movie. So far, this round was at a stalemate.

Hick: That one was too easy. Princess Bride. "I don't think it means what you think it means." Try this.

Annabeth studied the images for a moment. There were two faces with fangs and yellow eyes followed by an old fashioned fountain ink pen. She furrowed her brow and whispered to herself. "Twins... Two.... Dual Pen? No... those look a little monster-like." Then it hit her. "*Monsters Inc.,*" she murmured and smiled. She loved this game, and playing it with Hick made the distance lessen. She'd reply to the message later when she had another puzzle ready for him. That way, he would get it when he returned from his mission.

"Go on, dear."

Making up her mind, Annabeth climbed to her feet and leaned against her door. Pressing Hick's name, she chewed her bottom lip as she waited for his voicemail to pick up. Her breath hitched as she heard the bluesy sounds of Ray Charles warbling "Georgia on My Mind" wafting from the apartment next door. Hick used it as her ringtone ever since the night of Joselyn's wedding. One of her fondest memories was of him singing it to her in his rich baritone as they swayed across the dance floor at the reception. He had requested the tune specifically for them, and since then, it had become "their song." But, why would it be coming from Ms. Clara's place?

Her mental question was answered as six foot of muscular Navy SEAL, all dressed in camouflage and looking much sexier than a man had a right to, stepped out of the doorway. Dropping his duffle to the floor, he arched one sun-bleached eyebrow at her and winked. "Hey, Georgia, you've been on my mind," he growled sexily.

"Hick!" She screeched in shock. Then his arms

were open, and she leaped into them. Burying her face in the crook of his neck, she whispered, "I thought you weren't going to be able to get away for awhile."

Sliding his fingers through her red tresses, he placed a sweet kiss on her forehead. "We got some unexpected time for a few days, and I couldn't think of anyone else I would rather spend it with. Your neighbor saw me sitting out here waiting for you and came up with a way to surprise you. She was going to order a pizza and let me deliver it, but you seemed to need a little TLC instead. I hope that's okay?"

Normally, unexpected time meant something happened. Annabeth didn't ask because she knew enough that Hick couldn't tell her anyway. His missions were all highly classified and extremely dangerous. Instead, she rose up on her toes, planted her hands on his rugged cheeks and smiled through the tears that threatened to fall. "It's better than okay," she whispered.

"I'm sorry you had such a horrible day. I'm hoping I can make the rest of it a whole lot better?"

"It's already better," she murmured as she took in his features. Her heart was beating a million miles an hour and joy flowed through her veins. He had shown up completely unexpectedly. She knew she couldn't let her mind make more of it than just a booty call at best, but damn was she glad to see him. "If I had known you were coming, I would have rearranged my appointment and met you at the airport. You caught me with my drawers showing."

With a chuckle, he dove in and devoured her lips like he was dying of thirst and she was the last drink of cold water on the planet. Neither heard the door to Ms. Clara's apartment close. They were too lost in the moment of rediscovering each other. It had been too long since they had last been together and Annabeth's hands and lips were making up for lost time.

She was just about to say the hell with propriety and unwrap Hick right there in the breezeway of her apartment when the sound of a throat clearing on the landing broke them apart. With a sheepish grin, the management company custodian slipped by them and quickly had the lock fixed.

As Hick picked Annabeth up and walked her through the door with her squealing and laughing, she realized something fundamental.

Today was one of the best days she had ever had.

CHAPTER 2

The updated schedule of events arrived. Taking down the previous copy, the man tacked this one into its place. He studied it carefully and frowned. They would have to change the time by thirty minutes. It was a small adjustment.

29 days

Living the life of a Navy SEAL came with many perks and a few inconveniences. The one that most disappointed Hick was his inability to reset his internal alarm clock while on leave. Lying in bed with Annabeth's arm draped over his chest, her soft breath teasing his neck and her long red hair fanned out across the pillow, he grumbled at being awake.

He was bone tired after the mission in Brazil to liberate the missionary family held by guerillas in the jungle. They had gotten there in time to save them from physical harm, but the emotional damage was done, especially to their eight-year-old little girl. She refused to leave Cowboy from the moment he had untied her and picked her up in his arms for the trek back through the jungle. Afterward, she sat in his lap, clinging tightly with her blue eyes wide in fear as they evacuated from the area. She refused to leave him, forgoing even her parents' comfort. It was clear she equated safety with the former rancher from Wyoming. Once they were back in the States, the child had cried to stay with her hero. It had about broken the big man's heart to watch her leave, but that was a part of their job. However, it took an emotional toll on them, and nobody complained at getting a little down time even though they were still on call. Hick chose to spend his with Annabeth rather than visit his family in Boston or hang out in Cali. Getting lost in Annabeth's arms would always be the perfect vacation for him.

The first gray streaks of sunrise lightened the sky and peeked in through the mostly drawn curtains casting pink shadows across Annabeth's face. Looking over at the beauty beside him, he tenderly slid one strand of her crimson hair away from her face, marveling at his luck at having her in his life. Hick knew as a SEAL there wasn't a shortage of women who clamored for his attention. In the past, he had his share of one-night stands, and it had been fine; in fact, it had been preferable. A standing relationship had never been a priority for him, much to his mother's chagrin. Even though she had twin granddaughters, courtesy of Hick's younger brother, Elijah, she took every chance to remind him he wasn't getting any younger. With the announcement of his older sister, Antonia's engagement, he hoped to avoid more grumblings. Instead, it only made it worse.

Then along came Annabeth, his beautiful "Georgia" and changed all his perceptions. He remembered only too well how stunning she had been at River and Joselyn's wedding last year. He and Toad were flirting with a couple of bridesmaids when he caught sight of the curvy vision in a form-fitting teal dress with her mass of red ringlets pinned high on her head. He watched her closely as she moved around the room, talking to guests, running interference for the newlyweds and taking care of whatever task was necessary including cutting the cake. He excused himself from the ladies, leaving them in Toad's care and took the initiative to join her in handing out pieces of the confection. The gentle flirting turned into dances full of innuendos and eventually an unforgettable weekend in her hotel ordering room service and exploring each other intimately. It had ended too quickly for his liking.

A soft sigh followed by a movement from beside him brought Hick's thoughts back to the present. Leaning over, he gently kissed Annabeth's forehead and untangled himself from her embrace. She reached for him in her sleep, so he pressed his pillow into her arms and watched her snuggle up to it before succumbing to deeper sleep. Slipping from the bed, he threw on his workout clothes and went for a run. He may not have PT this morning, but it didn't give him an excuse to forego exercising completely. As a member of the elite Navy SEALs, he needed to keep his body in fine condition. Plus, he enjoyed the running. It gave him time to work out things in his head.

The "none" relationship with Annabeth had become so much more than he ever thought it would be. Given the fact they lived on opposite sides of the country, and both had jobs that made wrangling a relationship almost impossible, they mutually agreed to keep things casual. He had tried reverting to the fun-loving playboy he had been before, but it was no use. Since meeting Annabeth, every woman he met was a pale imitation of the vivacious woman that had stolen his heart that first night and held it hostage since. If only they lived closer together, he would convenience her they were meant for each other.

He frowned as he worked his way through the early dawn streets of Annabeth's neighborhood. Then again, he had an impossible job that threw a giant monkey wrench in the works. As it was, they had to be satisfied with a few stolen days here and there. Annabeth was funny, beautiful, charming, witty and so damned sexy. Everything about her intrigued him body and soul. However, this life was difficult on those kinds of relationships. While it was true he knew many SEALs with healthy ones; the odds were decidedly against them. As much as he would like a more permanent arrangement with Annabeth, he couldn't see dragging her into the uncertainty that it represented. As was par the course when his thoughts filled with the subject of their predicament, he found no solution for the situation.

An hour later, he returned to her condo and let himself in with the key she had pressed into his hand last night. "Just in case I manage to lock us both out again," she had told him with a glimmer in her eyes. The apartment was quiet even though the sun had already topped the skyline. Annabeth enjoyed her sleep time, and he'd kept her awake much later than she was accustomed to last night. He grinned broadly at the memory of their antics and a quote from one of his brother SEALs flashed through his mind. *You can sleep with a brunette, and you can sleep with a blonde, but take a ginger to bed, and nobody sleeps*. Hick snorted. Toad had a quote for any situation if there was a woman involved. He had a well-deserved reputation for being a man-slut; one of which he was insanely proud. Up until meeting Annabeth, Hick had admired the easy way his buddy could catch women. Now, it seemed lonely somehow, and he felt sorry for him.

At the thought of her name, the desire to rejoin her in bed overwhelmed him. Tamping it down, he reminded himself he needed a shower. There may be uncertainty about the distance between them normally, but he was here now, and he intended to make the most of it. That included taking care of his woman and making her breakfast. He sniffed his armpit and frowned. He was ripe - first a shower and then breakfast. Mustering his willpower, he bypassed her bedroom, grabbed his bag and hurried into the bathroom.

Standing in the kitchen twenty minutes later, Hick laughed when he opened the refrigerator. Inside were two eggs, a half a stick of butter, three sad apples, a bag of stale chips and a drawer full of brown sugar and vanilla candles. He never understood the reason for putting candles in the fridge. According to a Google search online it was supposed to make them last longer, but he wasn't sure he believed that. Wax melted when you burned it. What did the starting temperature have to do with it? Heat was heat.

The cabinet wasn't much better, but she did have some staples. She had once warned Hick she rarely cooked, and so kept very few groceries. Mentally taking inventory, he ran through the recipes in his mind and found one that was possible. Reaching inside, he pulled out flour, sugar, canned milk, and a few other items. That was joined by the eggs, butter, and apples that were just this side of turning bad, but he could salvage enough for his purpose. By the time she padded into the kitchen, yawning with her hair in snarled curls around her head, he had breakfast ready.

"Did you cook pancakes?" she asked sleepily.

"Mhmm. Here, have some coffee, and I'll fix your plate."

Annabeth poured a cup of the dark brew and dropped into a chair at her table. Hick set a plate stacked tall with brown syrup dripping down the side in front of her. Taking his stack, he sat beside her and dug in.

"Oh my God, what did you do?" she asked around a mouthful. "Is that apple?"

Hick nodded and swallowed. "Cinnamon apple pancakes with homemade caramel syrup. It's one of my favorites, and luckily, you had the ingredients but just barely. Your pantry looks sadder than mine, and that's saying something. At least I have the excuse of being out of the country a lot. You're here every day."

"You know I rather order out than try to cook. Gracie got the baking genes in my family. She's a lot like you - she can make anything. Honestly, I am shocked you found something edible. I hope you checked the expiration dates before using it."

"Don't worry, Georgia. I'm not going to poison

you. Enjoy your meal. The sooner you get done, the sooner you can get your work finished and the sooner I can have you all to myself."

With renewed vigor, she dug into the hot pancakes, stopping only long enough to swallow some coffee or to moan appreciatively. Out of the corner of his eye, he watched as she enjoyed her meal, finally pushing back the plate with a satisfied burp. Hick scooted his chair back and pulled her to him. Settling her into his lap, he wrapped his arms around her. She squealed and tried to get up. "Hick! I'm too heavy. I'll break your legs or at least a chair."

He snorted. "Woman, I've had to carry full-grown men for miles before. You in my lap won't hurt me. Besides, I like you where I can have my wicked way with you. Easy access and all that stuff."

She settled into his lap, wrapping her arms around his neck. "Have your wicked way, huh? What does that entail exactly?"

Hick's hand slid up from where it rested against her hip. Slipping it into the opening where her robe closed, he splayed his hand across her warm skin as he pressed nips and kisses along her collarbone. "A little of this," he whispered huskily.

He loved how her forest green eyes darkened to jade with the desire rising in her. She was so responsive to his every touch, letting him know in no uncertain terms how he affected her.

"A little of that."

"Hick," she whispered as her head fell back and he resumed nibbling at her neck.

Fire licked his blood when she clung to him with trembling fingers. She wanted him as badly as he did her. Well, who was he to deny them both what they needed? His fingers found the knot of her robe and deftly untied it with one hand. Slowly, he pulled the thick terry cloth material off her shoulder, peppering the creamy, speckled expanse with tender kisses. Nipping her playfully, he smoothed away the sting with more kisses until her fingers dug into his arm and she squirmed in his lap. He dipped his finger into the sticky remnants of his homemade caramel sauce and painted a line from her collarbone over the plump swell of her left breast. He felt her enflamed gaze as he licked the finger clean then dove in, tracing the path with his lips. As before, Annabeth squirmed and whimpered, arching against him and pressing her heated flesh to his lips.

"Please," she whispered, her voice going low and sultry.

Hick couldn't keep the smugness from his voice. "Please drive you insane? Yes, I believe I will."

She squealed as he made animalistic growls and pinched her skin with his teeth. Quickly, he shoved the robe down her arms until she was bared for his perusal. "So damn beautiful," his words were filled with heat. With a push, he sent the empty plates flying across the table to clatter to the floor spraying droplets of syrup everywhere.

"Now my floor is all sticky," she admonished.

"That's not all that's going to be sticky when I get through with you," he retorted. He picked her up as if she weighed nothing and sat her on the edge of the table amidst protests.

"If you break my table," she warned.

"I'll buy you another one. Hush, Georgia."

The satisfied smile his nickname for her brought to her face made him smirk. Quickly that smile turned to gasps and then moans when his teeth nipped at the tender flesh above her knee. He felt her fingers slide into his hair and hold on. She loved the little love bites almost as much as he loved giving them to her.

Her gasps and moans filled the air as he continued to tease her with lips and fingers until she was panting. Standing, he scooped her into his arms. "That table is a little too unyielding for what I want," he murmured.

She slipped her arms around his neck and laid her fevered cheek against his shoulder as he carried her down the hall to the bedroom. The sticky smack of his syrup covered footsteps was the only sound in the stillness of her condo until they were replaced with pleas then shouts at the culmination of their shared passion.

Annabeth watched Hick rinse the mop out from where he had just finished cleaning up their post-breakfast activities. Placing it in the broom closet, he emptied the bucket and washed it out in the tub.

"How long do you think you'll be?" he asked her as he stood.

She checked her makeup in the mirror and lifted her shoulders gently. "Couple of hours or less? It all depends on traffic. However, other than a conference call this afternoon at three with Joselyn and four of my other clients about the Phoenix convention next month, I should be free." She turned around and smiled warmly at him. "Think you'll survive that long?"

He sighed overly dramatically. "I guess so. It'll be difficult, but I think I can manage it."

She turned back to the mirror then leaned back as his strong arms wrapped around her waist.

"Careful, Hick, you squeeze anymore, and my girls are going to pop out and wave hello."

He laughed against her neck sending goose-bumps along her skin. "If they do, I'll kiss them good morning again."

She shivered. "Keep talking that way, and I'll not make it out of the house."

"I'm still trying to find something wrong with that."

The teasing made tingles of need slice through her blood. Swallowing, she forced her voice into a normal tone. "You make it hard for me."

Slowly he ground his hips against her. "No, baby, you're making me hard for you."

"Hick." Her breath became labored as her face flushed and her eyes fluttered closed.

He ran his palms over the swell of her cleavage. Finally, with a pained groan, he withdrew his hands and took a step back. Clearing his throat, he adopted a teasing tone. "Okay, enough primping; you're beautiful enough. I don't want some random guy to see my Georgia and think he can get her."

She laughed softly. This is one of the things she so enjoyed about him - his sense of humor and how he never failed to make her smile.

"Well that depends," she teased. "A girl has to hear all the options. If he can up the ante for all this hotness, I may have to trade you in."

He made a frown, poking his lip out. "Aw, now, Georgia. You're breaking my heart here."

She tried not to laugh, but it was useless. She broke into a giggle that became a full belly laugh. "Don't worry; most likely nobody can take your place."

"Just most likely, eh?" He growled and bit her ear, tugging it gently.

"Don't swallow my earring. They were my mom's, and I am not above dousing you with castor oil to get it back."

He laughed and started to tickle her. "Mean woman."

She squealed and pulled away. "Stop it, Hick. I have to go, or I'll be late."

He sighed dramatically but allowed her to pull away. He followed as Annabeth grabbed her cell off the charger and headed for the door. She stopped and turned, wrapping her arm around his shoulders and pulled him down. Cupping her palm against his cheek, she rose on her toes and kissed him gently. His arms twined around her as he pulled her tightly to him. The tender kiss turned passionate as he feasted on her lips until they both gasped for breath. She held on to him then reluctantly let him go.

"Take care, yeah?"

"Geez, Hick, I'm only going to be gone a little while. It's not like I'm going to drop off the face of the Earth."

"I know, Georgia. Just hurry so you can come back. While you are gone, I'll find another puzzle."

"I think it's my turn, isn't it? I haven't answered your last one. *Monsters Inc.*, by the way."

He shrugged. "That's good enough. You got it. Go ahead; I'll have to think of a good one and have it ready for you."

"I'm always ready." The twinkle in her eye had nothing to do with puzzles.

He groaned. "Georgia. You're killing me, babe."

Yeah, they were flame and gasoline when they were together, and it was obvious they both were pyromaniacs. The half-hearted smile filled her with longing to say the hell with the appointment and follow him back into her bedroom. Steeling herself, she instead turned away and opened the door. It took all her strength to walk away from him, but somehow she managed.

Moments later, as she flew down the interstate, her mind turned to the handsome man she had left behind. He had bulldozed into her life right as she had resigned herself to a being alone. There were other dates, but nothing that could be considered serious. Not that she and Hick were *serious*, exactly, but they did enjoy spending time with each other. He was funny, smart, sexy, passionate, hot.

So hot.

Lord, that man could melt a pair of asbestos drawers off a nun.

She shook her head and checked her speed. As was usual, when her thoughts turned to Hick, her foot tended to get a tad heavy. Easing up a bit, she moved into another lane and resumed her line of thought.

She and Hick had been seeing each other for just over a year. In that time, they had shared hundreds of Skype and telephone calls as well as more emails and texts than she could remember. Even though they had agreed to keep their relationship in the realm of friends with benefits, she couldn't lie to herself. What she felt for Hick went far and beyond simple friendship. She had been head over heels in infatuation with him almost from that first night. Whenever they managed to find time to spend together face to face, it got harder to part. Now he was here, in her home, and already she dreaded seeing him leave tomorrow evening. If she had known he was coming, she would have rescheduled today, but she couldn't do that on such short notice. On the one hand, it was just a couple of hours. She could get it done and get back to him.

Back to them.

Giving herself a mental shake, Annabeth turned her thoughts away from her very real feelings for Hick and onto the matter at hand. Today, she was giving a talk at the local community college on Artistic Representation. Sure, it wasn't glamorous, and there probably wouldn't be but a handful of people there, but she enjoyed sharing her passion with others. Not only that but she was thinking seriously about taking on an apprentice to help with the load. Her business was expanding at an unbelievable rate. She knew the recent success of Joselyn Chambers was a direct reflection of her abilities as an agent. What the two of them had managed together was nothing short of amazing.

As she pulled into the parking lot, her cell phone rang. Picking it up, she couldn't help but smile as

Hick's name filled the screen. Punching the button, she chuckled. "Can't wait for me to get home?"

The smile fell when she heard his pained tone.

"Hey. Georgia, baby, I've been called in. I'm sorry."

Swallowing hard she nodded, working to keep the disappointment from her voice. "Oh, when do you leave?"

"Now. I've got to report back in eighteen hours. The only flight out is in two hours." She heard the sounds of things being moved in the background. Most likely, he was packing his duffle bag.

"And you have no idea how long you'll be gone?"

"No, you know how it goes. It could be days or weeks."

Annabeth wiped at her eyes, and her voice dropped to a whisper. "Yeah, I know how it goes." Taking a deep breath, she let it out slowly then stiffened her spine. "You better take care of yourself, okay?"

The chuckle sounded forced. "You know I will. And Georgia? I did want to spend this time with you. Nothing less than my job would have pulled me away. You believe me?"

"Yeah, Levi, I believe you," she returned. "I'll talk to you soon."

"You bet you will. I'll text you when I can."

"I'll text back."

The line went dead, and she stared at her phone forlornly. In a quiet voice, she whispered, "I already miss you."

CHAPTER 3

A knock on the door caught the man's attention. With a grunt, he welcomed the intruder into his office. "Shipment," the newcomer reported then left. That should be the rifles, purchased on the black market. Thirty-six high powered guns complete with 2000 rounds each. He looked down at the desk and checked off another item.

24 days

"Whose turn is it? Please, don't say it's Hick's."

Reese "Toad" Harkins grunted. "It's Hick's."

"Didn't I tell you not to tell me that?" Alcide "Cowboy" Montgomery groaned. "I'll pay you fifty bucks to take his turn." He reached into one of the many pockets in his BDU pants, drew out his wallet and started to pull out bills. "I'd do it myself, but I've got duty. The only thing worse than his cooking is eating it cold."

Toad held his hand out and beckoned with his fingers. "Gimme. I'll open a can of beans for fifty anytime."

Hick reached over and snatched the bills from Cowboy's fingers with a grin. Folding them up, he tucked them into one of his brother's pockets. "Nah, you don't need to pay for dinner. I've got such a treat waiting for you, all of you will be begging for thirds."

"Dear Lord," Cowboy whispered. "The last time you said that I thought I was going to have to get my stomach pumped."

Hick stood and grinned at his fellow SEAL team members. "Don't worry, this will be amazing," he said with a wiggle of his eyebrows before he started to dig into the supplies stacked in the small shack they used as a base. Out of the six men that made up the SEAL team, Hick had the reputation of being the worse cook of the lot. The dishes he pushed at the others were at best indescribable and at worse, inedible. He snorted. If only they knew.

"MRE it is, then," Cowboy murmured as he pulled his pack over and rummaged inside.

"Yeah me too," Toad agreed.

"Already had mine," Hudson "Railroad" Houseman added. "Grab yours, Cowboy, and we'll go relieve the others."

"Aww, now, you guys are going to leave before chow's done? Suit yourself, that just leaves more for Bruiser and Finch," Hick pouted.

"We'll warn 'em," Railroad called out as he slung his pack onto his back. "They'll thank us for it."

Hick frowned as he glared at his friends. "You are going to hurt my feelings if you keep it up. I might stop offering to cook."

"If only we could be that lucky," Toad mumbled. He paused as Railroad threw his fist up making them all freeze in place.

"Company," Railroad hissed and disappeared out one of the windows.

As one, the three others adopted a stance of wariness, pulling their weapons around. A sharp whistle sliced through the room and they relaxed. "We were just about to come relieve you," Cowboy muttered.

Two figures materialized out of the darkness and stepped into the shack. “Hold up. We’re getting new orders,” the leader of their group, Grayson "Bruiser" Titus said as he dropped his pack to the dusty floor.

Standing, he walked out of the shack and into the darkness talking quietly into the coms, passing Railroad as he slipped back into the room.

Beside him, Finch glanced around. "What's for chow?"

"Hick," Cowboy and Toad said together.

"MRE it is, then," Finch returned.

"Fine. Enjoy your MRE's. One of these days you're going to be sorry you turned me down." Hick mock grumbled then dropped to sit on a thin wooden box propped against the wall. "I can turn anything into a work of culinary art, so don't whine if you miss out on a damned fine meal."

"We won't," the team replied together.

"Alright, listen up." Bruiser barked as he re-entered the hovel. "Intel for here is no good. Pack your gear. We're heading out in twenty."

"We're getting evaced?"

Bruiser nodded at Hick. "Yep. This mission is a wash. They don't think he'll be back."

Finch swore softly. "The bastard gets away again."

Cowboy slapped a hand on his friend's shoulder. "Look at it this way; we dodged another bullet. At least now, we don't have to deal with Hick's cooking for a while."

"True that," Railroad muttered as he settled his pack between his shoulders.

"If you're done, I'd like to get there sometime tonight," Bruiser barked.

Toad leaned in and whispered to Cowboy, "I think this time away from his lady is getting on Bruiser's nerves."

"After everything Livy went through, I can understand him being anxious to get back home."

Bruiser's fiancée, Olivia had been kidnapped from her job and trafficked to a sadistic pervert who took her to his private island in South America. It had taken the entire team working together to find and rescue her.

"Yeah, I guess you're right. I'm glad we were able to get Livy back. Did you see the news about that bust in Houston? I wonder if those eleven men were part of the same ring."

Cowboy lifted his shoulders in a shrug. "Who knows? I think Digger has been working on it but last I talked to him, he wouldn't comment one way or the other." Lifting the heavy pack, he slung it onto his shoulders and settled the harness comfortably. "I just hope every one of those bastards gets what's coming to them. I can't get the image of those poor women treated like animals out of my mind."

Railroad nodded. "That's one thing they have in common with ISIS. Maybe human traffickers and these terrorists are from different cultures, but they both think women are possessions to be pushed around and treated like garbage."

Finch settled his pack on his back, and double checked the area. His eye fell on the makeshift kitchen Hick was scrutinizing and shuddered. "You know, if we ever catch one of Fedora's lackeys, we could just force-feed him Hick's cooking. I bet he'd tell us anything we wanted to know."

Fedora was the code name assigned to terrorist Haafiz al-Bashir, the current number three on the ten-most-wanted-list. The U.S. government had been actively hunting him for most of the last year, ever since he began his current run of activities.

Toad snorted. "That would be considered cruel and unusual."

"If you two are through?" Bruiser raised an eyebrow at them.

With a mumbled apology, the men filed out of the tiny hut. Even as the inky blackness swallowed them up, they could hear Hick whisper, "One day you'll all be surprised."

"Yeah, surprised you didn't poison us," Finch grunted, and they all laughed.

Even Hick.

As their plane crossed over into American airspace, Hick slid his cell phone out of his pocket and powered it up. While the device cycled through its startup routine, he looked around the cramped space. Finch, Cowboy, and Bruiser had their phones out staring at the screens while Toad and Railroad dozed. Cowboy's father was going through a medical thing, and Bruiser was anxious to hear from his lady, Olivia. His worried face melted into smiles as a soft ding of stored text messages filled the space. In contrast, Cowboy's face turned into a frown, and he quickly dialed a number then walked off to talk in private.

The rectangle in his hand buzzed, and Hick let his eyes fall to the screen. Though they had been gone less than a full week this time, his Georgia had sent several messages. Quickly, he entered his code and started to read through their last exchange.

Georgia: Too easy. The Silence of the Lambs. 'Tell me, Clarice. Have the lambs stopped screaming?'

Georgia: Well, the class went well. I only had twelve attendees, but it seemed to go well. I hate you had to leave before I got home. Stay safe and talk to you soon.

Hick: Great news. Of course, it went well. You're awesome like that. Next puzzle?

A picture of a torn heart and a hilltop took up the next line from her.

Georgia: Levi Salter! I am very capable of buying my own groceries. You know I don't cook at home. What am I going to do with all this stuff that was just delivered? Wait until I get my hands on you!

Hick: I can't wait for you to get your hands on me. But the delivery - Most of that goes in your pantry. You know that empty little room beside your stove. It's for storing food.

Georgia: Ha, ha. 5,000 comedians out of work and you want to be one. Just answer the puzzle.

Hick: Too easy. Heartbreak Ridge. *Seriously, Georgia? That's one of my favorites. Clint Eastwood as a gunny sergeant. 'Jumping out of a perfectly good aircraft is not a natural act. So let's do it right, enjoy the view.'*

Hick: We're heading out. I'll get yours when I get back.

Georgia: You'll get my what, exactly? Just kidding. Keep your butt down and come home in one piece.

Hick: Will do. See you soon.

Georgia: What is baking powder and why do I need it? Where does it go?

Georgia: You know this stuff is going to go to waste? There's a reason my fridge is empty.

Georgia: I picked up a new client today. His name is Andrew Stinger, and he writes horror. Pretty fitting, don't you think? Stinger...Horror... He's self-published three novels over the past two and a half years and has gotten a fair amount of attention. Horror isn't my normal genre but how hard can it be?

Hick chuckled. He knew she hated horror movies and refused to watch them. He could almost imagine her sitting in the huge chair in her bedroom, lights all on with a blanket wrapped tightly around her as she reluctantly read Stinger's work. That was one thing he admired about her. Annabeth always made it a point to read every novel written by her clients, so she was well informed about plots, characters, and stories.

"Son of a bitch!"

Hick's head snapped up. Cowboy was pacing furiously in the tiny space. He stopped every few feet and slammed his fist into the fuselage. All attention turned toward their friend, even Toad and Railroad were awake, watching.

"You okay?" Bruiser asked.

Cowboy raked his hand through his hair. "Yeah. No. I don't know. Dammit!"

Bruiser stood and clamped a hand on his shoulder. "Your father?"

"Yeah. The treatment isn't working. Mom said the tumor is growing instead of shrinking."

"Damn. Anything we can do?"

Cowboy shook his head but looked at Bruiser. "She said they want to do surgery. I know this is a bad time with Fedora still in the wind, but do you think..."

Bruiser nodded. "Yeah. You worry about your Dad. I'll talk to Dixon and get the paperwork pushed through. You haven't taken any time off in a while, so I don't think this will be a problem."

Relief filled Cowboy's face. "Thanks, boss." He punched a few buttons on his cell and waited. "Hey, Ma," he spoke into the device. "I'll be there as soon as I can get everything squared away."

"Bruise? Can I talk to you a second?"

"Sure Finch, what's up?"

Hick turned his attention back to his cell and the messages Annabeth had left. She was so quirky and funny. She never failed to make him smile. As he finished, he checked the time. It was still early enough. He pressed the button.

She picked up the phone with a sleepy, "Hick?"

He chuckled. "Baking powder is made mostly of carbonate or bicarbonate and is used as a leavening agent. It makes baked goods rise and become fluffy."

"Uh, thanks? Are you home?"

He laughed softly. "We're back in the U.S., but I won't be home for a few hours yet. So, how're things? Staying busy?"

"Not too bad. You know, the normal stuff until the convention. Then it starts all over again."

"It's going to be in Phoenix, right?"

"Yeah." He heard rustling in the background followed by a yelp. Then a yell of, “Dammit, that's my toe.”

He laughed when she swore. “Good one. I’ll have you swearing like a proper sailor in no time.”

“Yeah, thanks but no thanks. So why did you ask me about where the convention was?”

"I thought that since you'll be so close, maybe we can get together."

He heard her voice hitch then she cleared her throat. "That depends. Are you going to buy a kitchen full of obscure cooking ingredients? Because if that's your plan, I'd have to bow out. When did you have the time to order all that stuff?"

Her exasperation was enduring. "I placed the order right before breakfast. I thought I was going to have a couple of days of pampering you. I had planned on making all sorts of stuff, but don't worry. I'll get my chance to cook for you soon."

Toad sat down next to Hick and pulled the cell phone from his hand. "Who are you threatening?" Putting the device against his ear, he asked, "Who is this and what did you do?"

"Give me my cell back. It's Annabeth." He grabbed for the cell, but Toad stood out of his reach.

"Annabeth? I thought you liked her. Why are you threatening her life?" He pushed a button and turned on the speaker. "Just say no, Bethy."

Her giggle erupted. "Hi, Toad. What can I say? I'm a glutton for punishment."

"Even a prisoner gets to be fed. And when I say fed, I mean things that are edible. Hick's food isn't anywhere near it."

"That's not true. He fixed me a lovely breakfast out of practically nothing. I'm still amazed at how he put together such strange things and making something that tasted great."

The look of alarm on Toad's face was priceless. "He fed you one of his concoctions, and you liked it?"

"It was delicious," she assured him.

Toad handed the phone back to its owner. "Well alright then. I've always heard when you find someone whose weird matches yours; you should hold on to them. There you go, Hick, both hands because she's obviously got an iron stomach and dead taste buds."

"It's not like that. Annabeth and I are just friends."

Toad snorted. "Yeah, sure, you fixed her breakfast which means you stayed the night. You call her as soon as we get back in the States. Every other thing is about her. It's pretty pathetic. Also, don't think we didn't notice you haven't dated other women since you two met last year."

Hick took the cell off handsfree and pressed it against his ear, ignoring his buddy. "Sorry about that, Georgia," he murmured. "That's just one of the disadvantages of spending so much time with this bunch. I have no privacy."

"Is what he said true?" Her voice had dropped until he covered his other ear with his palm to keep out the residual noise and hear her words.

"Is what true?"

"Is it true you haven't been dating since we met?"

Hick blew out a breath. How should he answer that? Their relationship was supposed to be light and unencumbered. He had thought about dating a few times but had given it up. How could any woman compare to his Georgia? But, if he told her how strongly he felt for her, it may run her off. Hick would rather have Annabeth in his life as a friend than not at all.

"Nah, he doesn't know everything. I've dated," he replied casually. "How about you?"

He heard the hesitation in her voice before she piped up. "Oh, yes, of course. You know how it is. I'm always so busy, by the time I get to a stopping place, I'm too tired to think straight." She paused. "In fact, Andrew Stinger has asked me out. Normally, I don't socialize with my clients, but he seems interesting."

Something ugly boiled in Hick's stomach and he gripped the cell tighter. After all, they were just friends, weren't they? Gritting his teeth, he forced back the green haze of jealousy. "That's awesome. I'm sure you'll have a great time," he answered evenly.

"I'm sure we will." She hesitated a bit. "It's almost midnight, and I have a nine o'clock meeting in the morning. I should be getting to sleep."

"Oh, yeah sure. So, take care, and I'll talk to you in a few days, yeah?"

"Yeah. Good night, Hick. I'm glad you made it home safe."

"Good night, Annabeth."

As he pushed the button to disconnect the call, he felt the sudden need to throw his phone across the plane. Instead, he pulled up a browser and did a Google search on Andrew Stinger. The thirty-seven-year-old author of horror novels had that intelligent, arrogant look that Hick equated with artists. His latest novel had hit several bestsellers lists, and he was recently picked up by a well-known publishing house. On paper, the guy looked great, and Hick couldn't fault her for wanting some stability in her life. That was something that he couldn't give her. Turning his phone off, Hick shoved it back into his pocket and leaned back. Closing his eyes, he silently cursed the situation. He wanted Annabeth for his own. He wanted it more than anything. He needed her in his life in a more permanent situation. However, the truth was the truth. Her job was in Atlanta, and his was in Cali. As long as he was in the SEALs, nothing could change. He had a minimum of another twelve years in the service before he could retire. By then, she would be past the age of having a family. Although she was a career woman, she had confided in him once that she wanted to be a mother someday and felt her biological clock ticking a little louder each year. He couldn't ask her to give up on her dreams of career and family to wait on him.

He knew all this, but it didn't help the bitter disappointment that filled his chest at the thought of his beautiful Georgia in the arms of another man.

CHAPTER 4

Twenty pounds of C-4 sat in the locked box under his desk. The shipment had taken longer than expected but it arrived well in advance. The maker would arrive in a few days. Payment was handled by order of the Left Hand.

One more thing completed.

22 days

Andrew pulled out Annabeth's chair and waited for her to sit. Once he had returned to his seat, he nodded at the waiter standing by to take their drink order. Without asking for Annabeth's preference, he requested two glasses of wine. He gave her a brilliant smile before dropping his eyes and studying the menu. Although she didn't know much about wine, it still irritated her that he took it upon himself to order for her. What if she wanted something else? Gritting her teeth, she resolved to just go with the flow. It was just a couple of hours, right? She could do this.

Annabeth wasn't sure exactly what had prompted her to accept Andrew's insistence on a date. He was handsome and extremely intelligent. However there was something almost devious in his mannerism, and that threw her off. She had adamantly refused his advances until Hick reminded her in his nonchalant way of his continued conquests. It had hurt more than she would admit to herself but it had been a wakeup call. She couldn't keep hoping that they could be more - that she could be more for him. So she called Andrew and accepted his invitation to dinner. Maybe if she told herself it was a business dinner, it would stop feeling so wrong to be here. She sighed heavily and concentrated on the menu.

The items listed sounded... strange. While Annabeth did travel extensively and tried many different foods, at heart, she was still just a little ole country girl from Georgia. She preferred more simple things that she could at least pronounce. Things like fried chicken, okra, potatoes with gravy and fluffy, homemade biscuits. Her nose wrinkled. What were chanterelles? Arugula she knew, but endive? Lord, she hoped that wasn't those raw peas that people liked from the sushi place. Lobster mushrooms made her giggle. She could envision the crustaceans lumbering on the seafloor with tiny little mushrooms dotting their heads like that character from the Mario video games. When she blurted it out to Andrew, he raised an eyebrow and smiled tightly then resumed perusing the offerings.

Chagrined, Annabeth settled on a dish containing pork belly and bean sprouts. That was bacon, right? Who didn't like bacon? Andrew ordered yellowtail hamachi that came with several fruits and something called ponzu. Wait. She thought that was a money-making scheme. She frowned. No that was Ponzi, wasn't it? Who knew ordering dinner could be such a questionable endeavor? She wished Hick was here to explain what all these different things were. He was extremely knowledgeable when it came to food and never steered her wrong. But he wasn't here, and after the last conversation they had shared, she wasn't sure when he would visit again if he ever did at all.

They gave the waiter their orders and settled into an uncomfortable silence. Annabeth fought to keep the sigh from erupting from her lips. Instead, she smiled at Andrew and broke the quiet. "So, how are you enjoying Atlanta? Have you gotten settled in yet?"

He took a sip of the wine that Annabeth found to be a bit too sour for her taste then nodded. "The real estate agent found the perfect home. I'm having some renovations completed that should be finished in about a month or so. In the meantime, I'm staying at a condo." He wrinkled his nose. "Thank heavens I'm not going to be there for long. It's not at all adequate for anything other than sleeping and dressing."

"I'm sorry you are having difficulties with the condo, but I'm glad the house coming along well for you." With the frown he gave her, she decided to change the subject. "Have you had a chance to check out the local sites? I just heard about Tiny Doors Atl. It's these little six-inch doors installed all around Atlanta by an artist named Karen Anderson."

"Why would anyone need a lot of tiny doors?" he asked scornfully.

She chuckled softly and leaned forward. "Nobody needs them exactly. The purpose is to inspire curiosity. What's behind the doors? Where could they lead?"

He shook his head. "I imagine they lead nowhere."

"You are an artist. Surely you can understand the desire to fill someone with imagination and wonder."

"Creating a 112,000-word masterpiece is not the same as gluing a miniature door on the side of something. If this so-called 'artist' wanted to create something magical, she could do much better than that."

"I suppose you have your thoughts. Personally, I want to spend one afternoon searching out all the doors to see them for myself."

He shrugged absently.

Sitting back, she wondered if things could get more awkward between them. In an attempt to re-engage in conversation, she tried again. "There's also Doll's Head Trail. I've seen that one, and it's fascinating. Artists have created many different scenes incorporating old doll heads. Maybe that would tease your curiosity?" When he stared at her blankly, she cleared her throat. "No, I guess not. Hmmm." Slowly she ticked off other offerings on her fingers. "54 Pillars, CDC Museum... Oh, wait. I know. You have to see the Adalanta Desert. I've seen it, and I'm sure it would be right up your alley. Geographer something that begins with a D created this fascinating intersection of alternative realities. It's almost like stepping into a book. There are plaques commemorating the crossing of two planes of existence. There's also a fabulous restaurant."

"I write horror, not science fiction."

Another deafening silence dropped on their table, and Annabeth fidgeted slightly. Desperate for a tension breaker, she turned the questioning to him. "So, tell me why you wanted to become a writer?"

The smile on his face was the first truly genuine one of the evening. Animatedly he began to speak. "To be honest, when I wrote *The Obsession of Veed*, I never could have thought it would become this thing it has. My parents were dismayed when I chose to give up my career to become an author full time. It was alright for me to dabble as long as I continued working at the firm. Now, don't get me wrong, I love architecture, but it isn't in my soul like writing is." He paused as the waiter refilled their glasses. He dismissed the man with a wave of his hand before continuing.

"When I told Father, I had gotten such a substantial offer for my current works along with a contract to produce six more over the next four years; he was flabbergasted." He leaned in and gave her a grin. "I'm afraid you are not on my parent's good list at the moment. The contract I signed a few days ago that you negotiated for me has sealed my fate so to speak. That, along with the trust fund left to me by my grandfather will ensure I don't have to go back to the firm unless I want. When Mother learned I was moving to Atlanta she about had a coronary." He shook his head with a wry laugh. "No, you are not their favorite person at all."

Annabeth slowly blinked in shock. His parents blamed her for Andrew's decision to leave Michigan? He had contacted her as negotiations for his literary contract started, but he had already done most of the footwork before she had become involved. Her influence was limited.

"Andrew, I hope you told them you had made these plans well before I came along? After all, your contract with me was signed only days before the publishing one. As a literary agent, my function is to represent you and your work in various avenues. In this case, I had practically nothing to do with your success. You were already coming here before my name was ever mentioned."

He waved off her concerns with a grin. "It's fine, Annabeth. They will get over it eventually. I chose you because of Joselyn Chambers. If you can get a mediocre romance author a two-movie contract, you should be able to do wonders with *my* work. Now that we are dating, you will work twice as hard to ensure your boyfriend is a resounding success. Of course, it won't hurt your reputation to be seen with me, now would it?"

What? She felt her face flush as realization dawned on her. Knowing he chose her because of Joselyn's success was one thing. For him to openly admit that he had only asked her out to cement his position in her hierarchy of clients was another. "Let's get one thing straight here. Just because I agreed to dinner with you does not put us into a personal relationship, and you sure as hell are not my boyfriend. As for your comment on Ms. Chambers, you have no rights to call her a mediocre romance writer. Joselyn is an awesomely talented lady and has worked hard to be where she is."

He chuckled and sat back. "I know it's hard work. I understand the difficulty in creating an entire world filled with different feelings and personalities. But, let's be honest here. She writes mindless dribble. It's little more than housewife daydreams. I've read her first book. I knew who the killer was almost immediately. Deidre, her protagonist, is one dimensional and is too enamored of John Michaels. He, on the other hand, is the perfect example of wishful thinking. Let's face it, Annabeth; a man who is as she described him would have little use for an imperfect, insecure, wall-flower unless it were to obtain a goal. My work, on the other hand, is much more cerebral. There's a psychological factor at play that forces one to think over every small nuisance. It's a huge difference. If you take out the fabricated chemistry between Deidre and John, there is nothing left of the mystery. I have to admit her sentence structure is excellent, and her ability to convey thoughts and emotions is first-rate, but the story and character development are extremely weak."

Annabeth felt fury burn in her throat. "Extremely weak? The chemistry between the two is multifaceted. He adores her. He is her perfect match. It doesn't matter what anyone thinks about how she looks next to him. They complement each other. They are a perfect couple, and the readers recognize it. They were voted the hottest fictional couple in a poll last Valentine's Day. Her characters are not weak."

"I didn't say they were weak; I merely stated the development was weak. There was too much hesitation between them. It became tiresome. Everyone knew they were falling in love. Get on with it!" He waved his hand dramatically. "That kind of writing is suitable for lovesick teenage girls and their bored mothers. If not for that demographic, nobody would have thought twice to pick up the novel."

Annabeth gritted her teeth. She was getting more and more pissed as each hateful, self-righteous word fell from his smug lips. Forcing down the blazing fire of indignation for her friend, she tried again.

"Joselyn Chambers's first book hit the New York Times bestseller list two weeks after it was released. That is a practically unheard of occurrence for a first-time author of any genre. She has put in a lot of blood, sweat, and tears to promote her book and get it seen by the right people not to mention she had to do it while hiding from a serial killer and rapist. The two sequels have each debuted on three major lists. Demma St. John is going to play the lead in the movie. It takes more than lovesick teenagers and housewives to get that sort of success."

"I know, and that is my point precisely. If you can garner that type of publicity for her, imagine what you can do for me? I have high expectations."

"Perhaps too high," she mumbled to herself. Taking a deep breath, she attempted to calm herself. "If you signed on with me expecting me to be able to create the same type of success for you then you may have made a mistake. I will represent you as best I can. I'll do everything in my power to foster your work in the best ways possible. However, Andrew, I thought for sure you understood I have no guarantees. Joselyn's success is her own. She earned it."

"My dear Annabeth, I'm not saying I want any guarantee that you will get me a movie contract. I'm simply stating that you have a talent when it comes to this business as evidenced by your ability to create enough excitement around Ms. Chambers to get her noticed. Once that happens, I can handle the rest."

Annabeth was shocked. Before she could retort, their waiter appeared beside them carrying a large tray. The meal placed before her was mostly plate and very little food. A slab of limp, soggy meat rested on top of a pile of grass with more cut grass sprinkled on top. The vegetables were strange, and she wasn't sure that she could stomach it after the bilge that spewed from her newest client's lips. It was one thing to lead his parents into believing someone else was to blame for his decision to move and quite another to openly trash-talk her best friend. Then add in his blatant admittance he wanted to date her only to further his career, and she was done. Placing her napkin on the table, she pushed back causing the chair to squeal on the tile floor.

Andrew glanced up at her as she stood. "Annabeth?"

"I think we should keep our relationship strictly professional," she bit out in an even tone. “I have a policy of not dating my clients to avoid any conflict of interest. I broke that because I thought you were a nice man. I was wrong twice over and will not be making that mistake again. There will be no more conflict because, brother, you are not interesting in that way any longer.” Picking up her clutch, she smiled tightly as all eyes in the room zeroed in on them. She started to turn away then looked back. "Joselyn Chambers may not write the same type of literature that you do, but she is a million times classier. You will never catch her saying snide, petty remarks about anyone else. In fact, in light of what you have disclosed, I am not sure we should continue in a working relationship either. As stated before, I will continue to represent you to the extent of our contract. However, I will remind you of the clause that states if a mutual agreement is reached in the failure of either party's expectation, the contract may be terminated with no adverse repercussions. Maybe you should think about that because I have to admit, my expectations have reached new lows," she stopped as their waiter hurried over, alarm on his face.

"Is there something wrong, Ma'am?"

She looked down at the food on her plate and nodded. "Yes, ya'll need to figure out how to cook bacon because this..." she motioned towards her untouched dinner, "this is not right; just not right at all. Enjoy your meal, Andrew. You can have mine too. Between the two, you may have a mouthful. Goodnight."

Turning on her heel, she strolled calmly out of the restaurant, ignoring Andrew's shocked calls of "Annabeth," until she disappeared out the door and could hear him no longer. She may be only a lowly literary agent and far beneath his ego, but she knew what she wanted in a partner, and Andrew Stinger was no Levi Salter.

CHAPTER 5

The man stared at the dispatch. An attempt had been made on one of the safe houses of the Left Hand. He snorted derisively. They would never catch him. The arrogance of these dogs will be their downfall.

22 days

The team had yesterday off after getting home so late the night before, but Hick hadn't been able to rest. Instead, he spent the entire day repainting the interior of the small bungalow house he owned near Ocean Beach. The rental on the apartment where he currently lived would be expiring soon. Hick wanted to be ready to move in by then. Besides, keeping busy kept his mind off Annabeth and he desperately needed a distraction from her. Ever since their conversation on the plane, he had a sinking feeling he was losing her and no idea how to fix it.

He had been so intent on finishing the painting that it was well after two in the morning before he dropped in the bed exhausted. Waking up after two hours of sleep for PT and work guaranteed today would suck and he had been right. Now everything was done, and he could finally go home.

"Are you going out with us?" Railroad stood from the table and pulled his keys from his pocket. "Bruise is going to Olivia's, Cowboy is packing for Wyoming, and Finch disappeared for his time off hours ago. That leaves you, Toad and me."

The thought of his sofa, a cold beer and the television called to him. He didn't even care to eat first, and that was saying something. However, going home didn't mean he would be alone. The ghost of Annabeth would haunt his thoughts until he finally succumbed to sleep sometime in the wee hours. Yeah, no thanks. Better to go out with the guys for a while instead.

"Sounds good," Hick answered dully.

"Aces or Dirty Dan's?" Toad had joined them and stretched. "There'll be more women at Aces, but the food is better at Dan's. Plus, Dan's is still quiet and small."

"And Dan will be at there as well. I've noticed you watching her, Toad. Be careful with that one. She'll tear you apart and lose the pieces," Railroad laughed. "She's not one of the normal barracks bunnies looking to make it with a SEAL. She owns the place and knows how to handle herself. I'd rather not get thrown out of there. They have the best-overloaded fries in town."

"And Danielle has the best body I've seen in a while. If I keep it up, my overwhelming charm will win her over eventually." Toad clapped his hands together. "So Dan's it is?"

Hick groaned, and Railroad shook his head. "Yeah, that'll work. But if we get banned, I'm coming after you."

An hour later, dressed in their civvies, the three entered the quaint little bar to find it hopping busy for a change. Railroad caught a rather harried looking Danielle's attention from behind the bar. She lifted a hand in a wave then went back to throwing drinks together.

"Standing room only," Toad grumbled. Together the three worked their way through the shoulder to shoulder crowd to the bar. Elbowing in, they waited to catch Dan's attention again.

"Hey Railroad, Hick, Toad. Crazy tonight isn't it?

Three on tap?"

They nodded as one and waited for their drafts to get there. Drinks in hand, Hick leaned over and shouted, "What happened? Not that I'm not happy for the success, but this crowd is intense."

Picking up her bar towel, Danielle pointed to a place on the wall behind her. Railroad read the framed print out loud. "The newest little sensation that nobody knows about, Dirty Dan's Pub has atmosphere, attitude and some of the finest food and craft beer you can find in San Diego." He grinned. "Congratulations, Dan. I guess those days of sitting and talking is over."

She barked a laugh. "I love the success, but I'm hoping it will tone down a lot. Ever since that article came out, I'm to the brim with college kids and yuppies out for an experience. That never was my target. I was thinking more of the neighborhood pub where friends could meet and spend some time together." She grinned largely, "And maybe pull in a few of the local hotties for eye candy."

Toad puffed out his chest. "See, I told you Dan likes me. She just called me a hottie."

"Oh, yes, of course, you too Toad. You're also welcomed to come around," she laughed at his put-on pout and turned back to help her harried bartender with orders. Beside him, Railroad and Hick roared in laughter.

"Shut down," Toad moaned. "My heart is broken."

"Got to *have* a heart to get it broken," Hick reminded him. "You've given yours away so many times there's no telling where it is now."

"I've loaned my body, but the heart is still safe." Toad patted his chest.

One of the tiny tables next to them paid their tab and got up to leave. Before the waitress could clear off the glasses, Hick was picking them up and dumping them into the bus pan beside the bar. Railroad snagged a bar towel to wipe off the surface and Toad dropped into a chair. Dan gave them a wink."Thanks, guys. First round on me," she told them over the crowd.

Railroad lifted his beer in a silent salute, and they settled in to enjoy a Friday evening. As was usual, it didn't take long before three women detached themselves from the crowd, sashaying over with sultry looks on their faces. "Heads up, here come the bunnies," he mumbled as he took a drink.

Toad sat up straighter and threw a smile on his face. "Ladies!" he called out. "Hello."

"Hi," purred a tall blonde. "I'm Brandy. The redhead is Sarah and behind her is Karmyn."

"With a K, not a C," piped up Karmyn, "and a y, not an e."

"Nice to meet you, Karmyn with a K and a y. I'm Toad with a T and a d, next to me is Railroad with two Rs, and across the way there is Hick - spell it like you hear it, plain and boring." He grinned charmingly. "Pull up a lap and let us buy you a drink. Something fruity unless I miss my guess."

Brandy giggled and turned to her friends. "I told you they were military. Did you hear the nicknames?"

Slowly, Hick closed his eyes. He was not in the mood for barrack bunnies tonight - the name given to women who chased military men to sleep with them. Instead, he drained the last of his beer and stood. "Here's a chair. I'm sure you can find a place for them to sit."

Toad snorted and pulled a pliable Brandy into his lap. "Yep, I've got a perfect place for you."

Sarah watched Hick for a moment then scooted around and placed a hand on his arm. "Are you alright?"

For a split second, Hick could almost see his Georgia in the woman standing beside him. They both had red hair, freckles, and deep green eyes. However, where Georgia had gorgeous womanly curves, Sarah was lithe and tall. The lack of a Southern twang was also obvious. This woman could never come close to the one who already possessed his thoughts.

"Yeah, I'm fine. Please excuse me, ladies. PT comes early in the morning." He pulled a bill out of his wallet and tossed it on the table. "The next round is on me. Enjoy."

Disentangling her hands from his arm, Hick gave the group a tight smile then worked his way out of the pub. Once outside, he took in a few deep breaths of the salty air then stuffed his hands into his pockets. Turning to the left, he walked away from the parking lot and stepped off onto the sand. Finding a bench, he dropped onto it and leaned back.

"She must be pretty special."

Hick's eyes flew open. Sarah stood by twisting her fingers nervously.

"Who?" Hick asked with a bit of confusion.

She slid her hands behind her thighs, flattening the slight flare of her skirt then sat down. "The woman that I'm not," she answered.

He pushed his hand through his hair. "Hey, I'm sorry. I didn't mean to be rude."

She laughed softly. "I didn't take any offense. I didn't even want to come out tonight, but Brandy guilted me into it." The salty air filled with the sigh of waves breaking on the shore before she continued in a soft tone.

"I saw you when you walked in with the other two. Brandy said she just knew you were in the Navy and probably SEALs. To let you in on a secret, Karmyn bet Brandy she couldn't bag one of you."

Hick let out a disgusted breath. "Well, if she's after Toad, she has a good chance. He's the poster child for man-ho anonymous. Railroad is a bit more reserved. He's particular about who he dates. And then there's me."

"The emotionally unavailable one," Sarah finished.

"It's that obvious, huh?"

She smiled and gave a little shrug. "Maybe just a little bit. I've been down that road before; trying to get back into the dating game while getting over heartbreak. Did something happen to her?"

"Not exactly. Georgia... I mean Annabeth lives on the other side of the country."

"And long-distance relationships are hard."

Hick didn't know why he was so forthcoming with what was going through his mind. Perhaps it was because of Sarah's resemblance to Annabeth or maybe it was the obvious concern on her face. Either way, it felt good to voice the uncertainty that plagued him.

"Yeah, really hard," he admitted. "We've been friends for a while now. With my job in the SEALs and hers in Atlanta, the logistics of getting together are almost impossible."

Sarah slid her foot out of the two-inch heels and buried her toes in the warm sand. Slowly she pulled them out, letting the sand trickle off the top. "My mother always said where there's a will there's a way. If you two want a relationship, then you'll have to work for it."

Hick leaned forward and braced his elbows on his knees. Staring out at the moon kissed waves, he considered her words. They had tried to work for it for a year now, but they were no closer to what he craved than the first night they met.

"She's on a date tonight," he said in a low voice.

"Ah. And you're not happy about that."

He looked at Sarah, but she kept her eyes on the breaking waves. "I want her to be happy. It's not fair to ask her to commit to me when there's so much working against us. She deserves better than that. I don't know what to do."

"Oh my God, are you serious?" Sarah jumped to her feet and glared at him. "Who are you to make that choice? You alpha males are all alike. You think you know what's best for others, but you have no clue." She started to pace slowly. "Here's an idea of what you should do. You should get your head out of your ass and talk to her. Why don't you call her and tell her how you feel?"

"And watch her run?"

Sarah snorted. "If she hasn't run from your career, then I'd say she thinks there's more than just friendship there. Seriously, what do you have to lose? You said yourself that there's a distance between you. You said the career makes things difficult. In my thinking, you're already experiencing the hardest part. Give the woman a chance to know her mind."

Her sudden outburst shocked Hick to his very core. This little spitfire stared him down as if daring him to take her advice. Suddenly he burst into laughter. "I think you just pulled my head out after all." He leaned back and pulled his phone out. He hesitated a moment. "What if she's still on her date? What if they are together?"

"What if she thinks you don't want her and you lose your chance?" She squeezed his arm and then slid on her shoes. "The world is full of what-ifs and antagonizing over them is just going to drive you crazy. I'm going to go find the others. Good luck, Hick."

He watched her make her way back to the raucous little pub down the street then stared at the screen in his hands. He made up his mind, pushed a button and waited for the call to connect.

"Hick?"

The hope in her voice was clear. With a smile, he replied, "Hey Georgia. You've been on my mind again."

Hick was calling her.

After the last conversation they had had, she wasn't sure how this would go. Then, he said those words that always made her smile.

"Hey. How are you?"

"I'm good. How was your date?"

The words came out tight as if he dreaded hearing the answer.

Letting out a heavy breath she blurted out, "It was a disaster. Andrew is an ass. I never even got to eat dinner. Not that there was much to eat anyway.

Why is it the fancier the restaurant, the smaller the portions?"

He chuckled; his laughter was rich and full of light-hearted mirth. "I've never really understood that either. When I'm hungry, I want to eat a full meal, not nibble on a sliver of meat."

"Oh, speaking of meat, I ordered the pork belly dinner. It didn't look anything like bacon. I like mine crispy, not thick, lumpy and covered in a bunch of grass."

"I'll keep that in mind. No lumpy, limp, bacon for my Georgia. Got it. I'll remember that the next time I cook you breakfast."

He called her his Georgia and was planning on fixing her breakfast. Suddenly the uncertainty of the last few days was wiped away. She relaxed and snuggled into the cushion and cradled the phone. They sat in comfortable silence for a bit. She could sit there for hours and not say a word, just be content to know he was there on the other side.

"Is everything going okay with you?"

She nodded then remembered he couldn't see her. "Yeah, all's good here. How're the guys?"

"Cowboy's dad isn't doing very well, so he's on leave to be with his family."

"Oh, I'm sorry to hear that. I'll be praying

for him."

Annabeth flipped off her television and curled up on her sofa. Snuggling down into her blanket, she felt the fear evaporate. "And the others?"

"Finch is on leave as well. I don't know what's going on with him. Bruiser is keeping his mouth shut about whatever it is. Bruise is so blissfully happy in love with Olivia; he stays with her as much as possible. Railroad is good, and Toad is his normal self."

"In other words, he's still womanizing," she guessed.

He laughed softly. "Yeah, pretty much. In fact, he was working on it tonight when I left the pub."

Annabeth felt her breath catch. "You were out at a pub?"

"Yeah, I was for a little bit."

"Oh." She chewed on her bottom lip a moment. "Do you want to get back to them?"

"No, Georgia. I want to talk to you. If I wanted to be in there with them, I'd be there."

"Really?"

"Yeah, honey." He blew out a breath. The line was silent for several moments. "Annabeth? Look, I think we need to have a long talk."

She felt her breath seize. Was this the end? Was

he tired of being friends? "A talk about what," she asked with a tremor in her voice.

"Oh, it's nothing bad. I think we need to discuss things; discuss what's going on between us. Talk about this thing that's between us." He stammered over the words. "Because where we are now isn't working."

She swallowed and clutched the phone tighter causing the plastic to creak. "You sound unhappy."

"I am, Georgia. But not how you think." He sighed heavily again. "I'm messing this all up. Look, I know you are busy but how about after Phoenix we take some time together. I'd like to see where we are and maybe, where we can be. I don't know how else to explain it."

Her stomach tied in knots. Was Hick asking what she thought he was asking? Was he seriously talking about something more permanent between them? Her heart leaped into her throat at the thought, and she swallowed it down.

"Georgia? You there?"

"Yes, sorry, I'm here. I'd like that a lot, Hick. I can't promise I won't have to work some, but most of what I do can be handled remotely. How long do you think you can get? I know you never know when you have to go and how long you'll be gone."

"That's true. But, if I'm not already on a mission, I'll take some leave. Okay?"

"Okay."

She relaxed. Hick was going to take some time for them to spend together. It sounded too good to be true.

"Alright, honey. It's getting late there. I don't want to keep you from your beauty sleep, although you don't need it."

She giggled at his words. "It's always better to be safe than sorry."

Softly she heard him sing to her with his deep sexy baritone. Her toes curled, and a huge smile brightened her face. "Georgia on my Mind" hadn't been one of her favorites until she heard him sing it. When he finished, she wiped a tear from her cheek. "Thank you, Hick. That was beautiful."

"Never be more beautiful than you, my sweet Georgia. Goodnight."

"Goodnight, Hick."

The line went dead. Annabeth hugged her phone to her chest and lay back on the sofa. Only three weeks until Phoenix then she could spend some time alone with Hick. It sounded perfect, and she couldn't wait.

CHAPTER 6

It was done.

The first strike in the glorious plan of the Left Hand of Allah netted the desired attention. The cell celebrated down in the living space. He allowed it, but he would not join them. As a trusted lieutenant of the Left Hand, he will not celebrate until returning home after the great plan was complete.

19 days

"Do you believe this shit?"

"Who did it?"

"Anyone claim responsibility yet?"

Hick stood in the back of the media center with his eyes glued to the screen. Dark smoke curled over a scene containing rubble, screaming and crying people and emergency workers. When he had awoken this morning for PT, the news of the bombing in Cannes was plastered on every outlet possible. Now he waited for official word of the event with his fellow SEAL teams.

The screen went dark as the briefing began.

"At oh-ten-hundred Zulu time, four vehicles carrying explosives targeted four buildings in Cannes including Palais des Festivals et des Congres. Details are sketchy at this time, but we're gathering intel." The Commander turned slightly and pressed a button. The screen flared to life once again. A woman's voice could be heard laughing then speaking in a mixture of English and French. The screen showed a beautiful avenue under a clear blue day. The area was filled with tourists going about their business. As the camera slowly panned around, a white van appeared on the screen, driving recklessly. The camera followed the progress with the operator commenting on the stupidity of people driving wildly in a busy area. The camera panned back to the avenue when there was an explosion. Smoke drifted upwards from a large building down the avenue. Three more explosions echoed in the air as people began to scream and run. The screen tilted crazily as the owner ran from the area before cutting to a different scene. In it, thick dark smoke filled the air and people were coughing. The camera panned around the area showing people walking in a daze, some with bloody places on their bodies. The scene stopped.

"This video was taken by a tourist during the attack. As you can see, there were four distinct explosions, all tourist areas. The Palais des Festivals was filled with people at the time attending a lesser filmmaker's festival. The body count at the moment is at 104 with hundreds more injured or missing. This message was sent to news agencies around the world."

The screen flickered on again, and a man wearing black robes with a ski mask stared blankly ahead. Behind him, the plastered wall was a dingy grey with many cracks like spider webs on the surface. He began to speak, and the translation flashed across the bottom.

Western culture is an abomination to Allah. No longer will we allow this corruption to influence the world.

"Same bullshit different day," Railroad mumbled from beside Hick.

"It sure seems that way."

"Shhh." Bruiser glared at them.

Hick turned his attention back to the screen. The terrorist continued to spew his hatred calling upon others to join in the jihad and bring down the West and America in particular. He continued to harp on how American values had corrupted the minds of the young and how American movies were violating the innocence of the world with sex and violence. His spiel went on for another ten minutes before he ended his tirade and the screen went blank.

"Because the terrorists mentioned American culture specifically, we have been put on alert. This is the same type of rhetoric Haafiz al-Bashir, code name 'Fedora,' has been spouting for the last three years. Although it hasn't been confirmed, it's believed he and his radical subgroup of ISIS are responsible." He clasped his hands behind his back and glared out of the gathered SEALs. "As you know, we have been actively searching for him. He is currently number three on the terrorist's most wanted list." The Commander stopped and wiped his face with his hand. Looking over the assembled, he continued. "This one bit us in the seat. There was no chatter on any of the usual outlets. With there being four bombs at once, we know there had to be some coordination. The question is how and where? The CIA, NSA, Homeland Security and a bevy of other acronyms is working to answer those questions. When those questions are answered, you can bet your ass we will be going after him. Therefore, all nonessential leave is canceled. Questions? Alright then, you're dismissed. I'd like to see the leads for each team for a few minutes."

One by one, the men filed out of the room. Bruiser, stayed along with the leaders of the other teams to speak with the Commander. The others left the building.

"How about lunch?" Railroad asked.

"Okay, sounds good. Hey, you think they'll call Cowboy and Finch back from leave?"

"I dunno, Toad. They said nonessential leave. I guess it depends on why Finch is gone and if they think cancer surgery on Cowboy's father is essential." Railroad glanced over at Hick. "How about you? Get some chow?"

"Nah, you go ahead. I've got something to do."

Toad snorted. "Tell Bethy hi from us."

A growl erupted from Hick. "Her name is Annabeth. Don't call her Bethy."

"Says the man who calls her 'Georgia.' At least my nickname is close to her normal one." Toad smacked Railroad on the shoulder. "I told you he was serious about her. You owe me a twenty."

"Bite me. I'll buy your lunch, that's the best you get. See you later, Hick."

The two walked off toward the parking lot leaving Hick alone. He pulled out his cell and punched Georgia's number.

"Hey, you."

He couldn't help the grin that split his face. "Hey, Georgia, how are you?"

"Better now. I took today off and went to Chattanooga to visit my sister. It was time for a little nephew therapy."

"Is that the mysterious man that has you all flustered?"

Hick laughed as Annabeth hissed at her sister. "Would you hush? He can hear you."

Annabeth's sister, Grace, called out, "Hey Hick! When are you going to visit? Elliot can't wait to meet you. He calls you Uncle Hick."

"Ignore her," Annabeth muttered between gritted teeth. He could imagine her cheeks turning red. She was so cute when she got embarrassed. The flush started at the top of her face and rushed down to disappear into her shirt.

"Uncle Hick, huh?"

"He's only six," she said defensively. "He's never even met you. But when he overheard me telling

Grace that you were in the Navy he got excited. Now he wants to be a soldier or a bartender. And before you ask, he saw Tom Cruise flipping bottles in *Cocktail* and thought it was cool."

Hick erupted in laughter. "Well, I don't know if I can compete with Tom Cruise."

"You're better than him any day of the week."

"Well, I do try."

She hesitated a minute. "Hey, would you mind facetiming with me a few minutes? Actually, I was hoping you would talk with him. It would thrill him beyond words."

"Sure. Let me call you back. I'm on the way to the parking lot."

He hung up then jogged to his car. Once he settled in, he called her back using the video application.

"H-h-hello?"

A little boy's face filled the screen. He had the same red hair as Annabeth and a smattering of freckles across his nose. However, his eyes were a clear light blue instead of dark green. No doubt, he took his eyes from his father, who worked in construction.

"Hey, Elliot, I'm Hick. How are you?"

His blue eyes lit up, and a smile erupted on his

chubby face. "Hi, Uncle Hick. I'm fine. Are you on a boat?"

He shook his head slowly. "Sorry, buddy. Not today. I'm sitting in my car." He moved the camera of the cell around slowly and showed the boy his surroundings.

"Oh." Elliot's face fell. "I like boats. We got to ride in one at Disney. There were pirates. Do you have pirates?"

Hick's heart stuttered slightly. The innocent questions were so endearing. "No, we don't have pirates here."

"That's ok. One of them said they wanted the redhead, but I wasn't scared. I protected my mom and dad just like a real soldier."

"You did well. I'm proud of you."

Elliot nodded absently. "You can talk to my Aunt now. It's time for Batman on television. Bye, Uncle Hick."

"Bye Elliot."

The scene juggled then his Georgia filled the screen. As expected, a slight flush still stained her face. "Thank you for talking to him."

"Anytime."

He watched as Annabeth made her way out of the house and sat on her sister's porch. In a small voice, she said, "I know you can't talk about it, but is everything okay there? I mean with the explosions this morning."

"Yeah, it's all fine." He could hear how tight his voice was. It wasn't exactly a lie. He was fine, but that could change at the drop of a hat.

"Okay." She chewed her lip. "Are we going to be able to see each other in Phoenix?"

"Hopefully so, but I can't make any promises. You've seen how things are with us. We never know what's going to happen from one day to the next. But, the only way I'm not going to have you in my arms again is if I'm physically out of the country. Nothing else is going to stop me." He hesitated a moment then shoved one hand through his shaggy hair. He didn't want to scare her, but it was time to lay down the foundation. "I know I told you I wanted to have a talk with you when I get there, but I need you to be thinking about something. We've been doing this friends thing now for a while, and I think you know as well as I that there's a lot more than that between us. I want you to be thinking about us and what you desire because I've thought of little else the last few days. Then as soon as I can figure out the logistics, either at the convention in Phoenix or soon after, we are going to sit down and discuss this thoroughly. Okay?"

Her eyes had gotten as big as silver dollars, and she nodded slowly. "Okay," she whispered and bit her bottom lip. "Yeah, I'd like that."

"Good." The relief he felt was palpable. At least she was open to talking their relationship through. He watched her through the screen and wanted to reach out, touch her face and feel her cheek beneath his fingers. He longed to gently tug her lip out from where she was nervously chewing it and nibble on the plump pillow himself. With a groan, he closed his eyes. Lord, what she did to him and she wasn't even in the same part of the country!

"Are you alright?" Worry etched on her face.

He coughed. "Yeah, I'm fine Georgia, but do me a favor. Stop biting your lip. It makes me remember how you taste and I want to take a nibble for myself."

She tittered then blushed again. "You're in a weird mood today."

He frowned. "What do you mean 'weird'?"

"You seem serious like you aren't just teasing me."

"I'm not. That's part of what we're going to talk about, just not here and not now. I need to be face to face with you."

There was a shout from behind her, and she

turned to speak with Grace a moment. Turning back, she sighed. "I have to go. Grace needs my help catching a spider, or she won't go back to her kitchen until Kenseth gets home tonight."

"That's my brave Georgia, saving the day."

She rolled her eyes. "Your Georgia was promised fried chicken, black-eyed peas, and peach cobbler. That's not happening as long as a spider holds the kitchen hostage. I have ulterior motives."

"Alright then, go save dinner. Let me know when you get home so I won't worry."

"I'm a big girl. I'll be fine."

"Humor me, Georgia. Please?"

She nodded then stood. "I've got to go. I'll talk to you soon."

"You sure will. Bye."

The screen went blank, and Hick sat back, leaning his head on the headrest. He had to admit it; he had it bad. Georgia was everything that was good in life, and he had to find a way to fix this distance problem between them. If not for any other reason, his sanity demanded it. Annabeth Switcher was killing him, and maybe it made him crazy too, but he wanted more. He laughed. Well, at least they would be crazy together.

He hoped.

CHAPTER 7

Amir stood in the man's office with a smile on his face. The American had proved himself and the Left Hand had decided to give him the honor to complete the plan. The man didn't care, as long as he didn't mess it up. There was too much at stake.

17 days

Annabeth sat on the balcony of her condo and sipped on her iced tea. The view was one of the things that had sold her on this particular location, and she loved it. The lights of the city reflected off the lake in Piedmont Park making tiny glittering stars in the water. Overhead, though they were dimmed, the real stars twinkled. She sighed happily and stroked Precious sitting on her lap. There were times that Ms. Clara's animals made Annabeth want to scream. However, when they weren't digging up her ferns hanging around the small space or trying to scratch the fabric off her chaise, she enjoyed their company. Like now, when she was contemplating how her life had changed in the past few years, her fingers slid through the cat's fur absently. The repetitive action calmed her.

"You've been quiet lately."

She greeted her neighbor as she continued to stroke the velvety length of Precious' back eliciting a deep purr from the feline. "I've had a lot on my mind. My new client is a jerk, and my best friend is off in Hollywood, consulting on a movie script. The biggest book convention of the year is coming up in a few weeks."

Ms. Clara sat down on her side of the balcony and sipped from a delicate china cup. Placing it back on the small table at her side, she stared out over the view. "And, it doesn't help that today is their anniversary."

Annabeth's head whipped to the side. "I didn't know you knew."

The older woman's chuckle filled the air. "It's only been three years. My memory isn't that far gone yet. You had only moved in that year. It was before

Stinky and Popcorn passed away. Those two spent more time over here than the others."

"I remember. That was before you got on the Tolkien kick."

The two sat in silence for several moments before it was broken by Ms. Clara. "I know you miss them."

"I do. Not a day goes by that I don't wish I could talk to Mom again. I can't watch any old movies without thinking about Dad. That was our thing - watching old movies together. There are so many memories that are tied up with everyday things. I've been told that time heals all wounds, but not this one. This hurt is in my very soul and just as raw as the day I kissed her cheek and told her I loved her as she slipped away."

The skyline became watery as Annabeth watched the dancing lights. She didn't bother wiping her eyes as her heartbreak dripped down her face.

"I have always had a fierce independence streak; sometimes, it was almost too fierce. Momma and Daddy were both blue-collar workers right here in Atlanta. Daddy worked night shifts for a local manufacturing company as the head of maintenance and Momma was a beautician in a downtown salon.

Because of that, Grace and I had to fend for ourselves a lot of the time. Grace is six years younger than me so it was up to me to keep her entertained. We got a small allowance as kids, and we saved them up for trips. Ten dollars a week turned into adventures once a month. We figured out the Metro schedules before I could drive. Ballgames, the Aquarium, concerts... you name it, and we did it. Atlanta was our playground. When I got my first job, then I could pay more for us. One year, I bought us season passes for Six Flags. That summer, we spend every moment we could there. Sometimes, Momma and Daddy would go but it was mostly just Grace and I. They were too tired to go and do after working so hard."

Ms. Clara said nothing, simply listening as Annabeth talked.

"We had a great childhood. They weren't there a lot, but the house was filled with love. Momma left for work at six to beat the almost two-hour commute into the city just as Daddy made it home from his twelve-hour shift. They were two ships in passing, and Daddy often joked it was their crazy schedules that insured they had a happy marriage. They were never home together enough to fight." Annabeth smiled at the bittersweet memory. "When they were together, it was more than obvious how much in love they were. Perhaps having so little time to spend together insured that the time they did have was precious. Then Daddy was diagnosed with stage four lung cancer. I remember that day so well. We all thought it was bronchitis again. He smoked like a chimney, but his cough was so much worse than normal. We had dinner together that weekend. Afterward, we were sitting on the sofa, watching Elliot play on the floor, and Daddy just blurted the news out. We were floored. 'I have cancer, and it's bad. Now, I'm not going to give in. I intend to fight, but they only give me three months. You girls have to promise me that you won't give in either. This family has been through a lot, but together we are strong.'"

Annabeth stood, causing Precious to jump down and saunter into Ms. Clara's lap. Stretching, she curled up into a ball and resumed her nap. Her mistress said nothing, simply running her gnarled fingers through the silky fur.

"Momma retired from her job and spent every moment taking care of him. He lived another six months past the prognosis. Grace says it was pure stubbornness. He was a shell of the man he had been. We made a bedroom out of the dining room, so Momma didn't have to go up the stairs to sleep. I remember the sounds of the machines that supplied air for him and the smell of antiseptic covering everything. His oncologist wanted to put him into a care facility, but Momma said no. She wanted him with her, in the home they built together." She swallowed as the painful memories made her throat close. After a moment, she continued.

"Grace was in the kitchen, washing dishes after dinner. Momma was half lying on the bed, watching the news and I was sitting there, holding his hand when his time came. He just breathed his last, and she kissed his cheek and told him she would see him again one day. It was all so bittersweet. One minute he was there, then he wasn't."

Annabeth shook herself. Wiping her fingers over her damp cheek, she whispered, "Momma had a massive stroke exactly five weeks after his death. She lived long enough for us to get to the hospital to tell her goodbye. We buried her next to him. To this day, we believe Momma grieved herself to death. She just couldn't contemplate a life without her soul mate. She told him she would see him again, and that was a promise she intended to keep. Now Grace and I only have each other."

"Ah, I had wondered. Now I understand."

Annabeth's brows wrinkled. "What do you mean?"

There was a creak as Ms. Clara slowly rose to her feet. With a shuffling step, she made her way to the small gate that separated the two sides of their shared balcony. Gripping the railing in her hands, she leaned forward.

"I wondered why you stayed in Atlanta. At first, I thought it was your job, but you told me most of your clients are in other cities or even states. Then I thought it was because of Grace, but she moved to Tennessee. I know the lease here is year by year, so that isn't it."

Her too bright eyes seared Annabeth as she talked. "But now I see. It's fear. You're afraid of forgetting."

"That doesn't even make sense, Ms. Clara."

"It makes perfect sense." She lifted one shoulder in a half shrug. "Atlanta is your home; it's the place that holds so many memories for you. The house where you were raised, the places you and your sister visited together. It represents safety and a thousand memories that make up your past. It's the connection to your parents."

"I guess so."

"There's no guessing about it. Let me ask you something, and I want you to think hard about your answer. What about your Navy young man?"

"Hick?" Her head shot up, and she stared at her neighbor. Where had that come from?

"Yes, Hick. What about him?"

"I don't understand."

She barked a laugh. "You understand; don't play possum with me."

Annabeth felt her cheeks redden. She was asking the question that had been on Annabeth's mind constantly. Where did Hick fit into her life?

"He's my friend."

"Horse pucky! I may be an old woman with old eyes, but I can see what you obviously can't or won't." She opened the gate and walked through then sat on the end of the chaise Annabeth had vacated. Pointing her finger at the younger woman, she narrowed her eyes. "He's head over heels for you and you for him. It's clear enough for a blind man to see."

Annabeth laughed uncomfortably. "Oh no, you have it all wrong. We are friends." She remembered the hints he had given her that he wanted more. She warmed at the thought. "Or at least that is all we have time for right now. Even if it could be more, it's not exactly an ideal situation we are living."

"There's always time; you just have to find a way

through. Your parents worked opposite shifts but still found time to have a family and a life together."

"They lived in the same house."

"And yet, they were still apart. Sleeping in an empty bed is still an empty bed. Being in the same house is just geography. However, they still were able to have a beautiful life together with you and Grace."

"But his job is dangerous," she cajoled.

"Every job has its dangers," Ms. Clara retorted. "My Henry was a luggage handler at the airport for twenty-eight years. After the first three, I asked him not to tell me how many times he'd almost gotten killed on that damned tarmac. James works in accounting in Philadelphia. You'd think that was safe, wouldn't you? They replaced some windows on the building he worked at, and one of them crashed to the sidewalk six inches behind him as he walked to lunch one day. The wind of it almost knocked him down. Even your job is dangerous. You fly all over the place several times a year. I worry that you will be on the wrong flight some day. Your job is dangerous too."

"Jeez, please don't speak that into being!"

Ms. Clara chuckled, "I'm just reminding you that life is short and nothing is guaranteed to us. You need to find the little things that make you happy and hold on to them with both hands. Henry left me at fifty-three. We had thirty-five beautiful years together, and I wouldn't trade one of them for all the tea in China. Do I wish there were more? You bet your bumpkus. When he died, I thought my insides had frozen over. I had to find a reason to wake up each day. I had to find a reason to live again."

"What was it?" The story spellbound Annabeth.

"James," Ms. Clara finished triumphantly. "And Henry."

She wrinkled her brow. "Henry?"

"I had to live for him too. Because of those memories we shared and the life we had. I owed it to him and to me to carry on the life we had together. It's hard. Some days it becomes so hard I feel it like a huge boulder on my shoulders. But I remember Henry's smile and I pick myself up and keep going. I do it for James, Mara and the grandkids. Who is going to tell them what a wonderful man their grandfather was? But the point here is love is a beautiful mess, and you are lucky to find someone who wants to spend their life with you."

Annabeth shook her head, "No, it's not like that. Hick is a free spirit. He has to be in California. When they call, he has to go. He has enough to worry about without throwing me into the mix."

"You're already in the mix." Ms. Clara studied Annabeth's face then continued. "The day he had to leave when you were at work, I sat there on that balcony and watched him. He was sitting right here, where I am, staring out over the lake. He didn't know I was there, and I didn't mean to eavesdrop, but well, I'm a nosey old woman, so I didn't say anything. He talked to you and how sorry he was that he couldn't stay longer. He spoke about things that I'm not going to talk about because it's not my place. Those things should come from him. I think you need to hear them with an open mind and an open heart."

Something warm bloomed in Annabeth's stomach. She craved to know what Hick had said when she wasn't there. A niggling voice in her heart told her it was going to be very important. Even though she knew he was in a four-day training exercise, she longed to hear his voice.

"Maybe I should call him."

Ms. Clara climbed to her feet and nodded. "Maybe you should. And Annabeth, take some advice from an old woman: it's okay to remember and honor the past, but don't live your life in it. Your sister doesn't need you taking care of her any longer. Your parents are together for eternity. None of them would want you to pass your happiness by to hold on to something for them."

"Yes, ma'am," she said absently as she reached for her cell. She didn't notice as the old woman shuffled through the gate and into her own house. Instead, she waited for his voicemail to pick up.

Levi Salter. Leave your message, and I'll call when I can. If you're calling from Publisher's Clearinghouse, I'll take the lump sum. If you're from the police, I can explain. Probably. If it's a gorgeous redheaded literary agent with killer curves and the most beautiful smile who lives in Atlanta, hey Georgia. You're never far from my mind and don't believe anything Toad tells you. He was drunk. Or maybe I was? Anyway, here's the tone.

BEEEEP

"Dear God," she muttered but smiled.

CHAPTER 8

The second tip of Allah's spear went off with no problem. Now they were next. Tension built in the air as every man felt the weight of their mission.

15 days

The training exercise was brutal.

For the past four days, Hick's team along with the one headed by Matthew "Wolf" Steele had lived, slept and worked in the Mojave going through different scenarios as intelligence was gathered on the mastermind behind the Cannes attack. As they had guessed, Haafiz al-Bashir, AKA "Fedora" had claimed responsibility. It was time to take him out.

Their combined team had been designated as Bravo while another combined team was Alpha. For the last exercise, Alpha had played the part of the terrorists with Bravo mounting an assault intent on bringing them down. They had played this war game over, and over the last forty-eight hours, trading sides as the one tried to figure ways to stop the other.

"Damn, I'm exhausted," Mozart muttered as he dropped to the ground beside Hick. The SEAL, also known as Sam Reed, shrugged out of his pack and leaned back against the rock and closed his eyes. "I'm ready to get out of here and get home."

"Me too. Jess wasn't feeling too hot when we left. I need to get back to her." Kason "Benny" Sawyer dropped beside his friend.

One by one the other members of Bravo joined them on the hard sandy ground as the sky overhead darkened toward blackness; all except Finch, Wolf, and Bruiser. The two leaders were off to one side talking quietly together. Finch sat on a boulder staring up at the sky as the stars began to show. He had appeared as they were loading up to leave for the training exercise. He looked drawn and barely spoke. Hick had no idea what had happened to him over the last week, and he wasn't forthcoming with the information. Bruiser obviously knew, but he was just as tight-lipped stating if Finch wanted to talk about it, he would.

"We're out of here tomorrow, right?" Toad asked.

"That's the plan, Stan," Railroad grunted. He sat against a boulder with his rifle lying across his lap.

"Can't come too soon for me," Hunter "Cookie" Storm retorted. "I want a hot shower, a warm meal, and my wife."

"How's she doing?" Hick asked. "I heard she had been having some issues."

Cookie nodded. "Fee's doing better. The new therapist has helped a lot. After that piece of shit, *El Chacal* came after her, I was afraid she'd break, but she didn't. My Fiona is strong."

"Damned strong," Dude grunted. "All our women are - Ice, Fiona, Alabama, Summer, Jess, and Shy. Every one of them went through hell and came out on top."

"They have to be strong. It takes a special woman to be with a SEAL," Abe added. "It's not easy."

Hick straightened up. "Does it work? I mean, it obviously works because you are all still with your women. But, the distance, the missions, how does it work for you? How do you keep your mind on the mission?"

Cookie blew out a breath. "You learn to compartmentalize because when you're on a mission, not having your head in the game can get your ass killed. It can get your team killed. Believe me, I know. It almost happened to me."

"And me, " Abe added. "She's there, in my heart, but I push her out of my mind while working. You have to. I remind myself that I'm doing this for our country; for every man, woman, and child. I'm doing this to ensure Alabama, and our kids are happy and healthy. No, it's not easy to leave her and go God knows where with no assurance that any of us is coming out of this alive, but we go because it's what we are."

"Not to mention homecomings are pretty freaking awesome," Benny grinned.

"True that." Mozart fist-bumped Benny.

"You got a woman, Hick?"

Hick resisted the urge to fidget under Dude's intense stare.

"Depends on what day it is," Toad grunted. "Bethy deserves better, but for some reason, she's stuck with him."

"Annabeth is my friend," Hick replied as Railroad, Toad and even Finch snorted. While it was true that he wanted more and he was sure she did too, he wasn't ready to share it with the team.

"Man, when are you going to wake up and smell what you are shoveling?" Toad reached over and slapped Hick's helmet off his head. "You two have been dancing around each other for almost a year now. It used to be funny. Now, it's just sad and a little disgusting."

"Shut up, Toad." Hick grabbed his gloves off his thigh and threw them at his friend, smacking him in the face with them. "It's not sad or disgusting. She lives in Georgia, and I'm in Cali. The timing just isn't right."

"Riiiiiight," Toad picked up the gloves and tossed them back. "You spend more time on the phone with her than Bruise does with Olivia and they are practically married. You two send those little text games back and forth all the time, and if you are within 500 miles of her, you find a way to see her. If that's not sad and disgusting, it's pretty pathetic at least."

Railroad jumped to his feet and tilted his face to the sky. "You hear that?" he asked.

As one, the rest of the team immediately fell silent. Standing to their feet, they listened as a noise began to grow.

"Helios?" Mozart frowned.

Twinkling lights moved through the darkness from the west. Wolf and Bruiser joined the men.

'Get your gear. We're being pulled early," Wolf ordered.

"What's going on?" Finch asked as he settled his pack on his back.

"There's been another attack. Fedora has struck again," Bruiser growled.

Details are starting to come in from Novi Sad, Serbia at the Exit Festival. The music festival, founded in 2000 by students to protect democracy in Serbia, was the site of a terrorist attack tonight. The American band, Brown Nugget Toast had just taken the stage when four explosions rocked the Petrovaradin Fortress collapsing two walls of the medieval structure trapping thousands beneath the rubble. Reports of casualties number in the thousands with the death count at 149 and climbing. Haafiz al-Bashir claimed responsibility via a message released immediately following the incident. In it, the spokesman railed at Western culture including American influenced music. In his speech, he called for Muslims everywhere to stand with them in their holy war.

Annabeth's eyes were big as saucers. She scooted

to the edge of the sofa and watched as the scene unfolded before her gaze. As at the last attack, smoke hung thick in the air as terrified people stumbled around in shock. Officials had arrived, and efforts were underway to get the situation under control. Local news reporters gave their reports as machinery and people swarmed the scene behind. English translations flashed across the bottom of the screen.

A vibration pulled her attention from the screen. She picked up her cell and answered.

"Hello?"

"Hey, Georgia."

Never had two words sounded so good to her. "Hick! God, it's good to hear from you."

"Good to hear from you too." The sound of the mouthpiece being covered as he mumbled something then he was back. "Are you doing okay there?"

She nodded then remembered he couldn't see her. "Yes, I'm alright. Hick, what the hell is going on? Who is this guy doing all these bombings?"

She heard him sigh heavily. The sound of a car door opening was muffled in the background then the door slammed. "He's a bad man. No, bad isn't the right term. He's evil, plain and simple. Al-Bashir is an egotistical extremist with dreams of bringing down anything that he doesn't believe in or understand."

"Why does he keep targeting artistic locations? I don't understand."

"I wish I could give you an answer, Georgia. These extremists don't care about anything but their agendas. They warp the true Muslim faith into a tool for hate and lies. Millions of believers don't subscribe to the viewpoint of these terrorists. They are just as much a victim here as those who are physically hurt. These fanatical bastards view our way of life as a direct affront to their skewed religious beliefs. To them, it's sacrilegious, and their version of God demands justice."

Annabeth shivered as she rubbed her hands up and down her arms. "Any god that demands justice by killing thousands of innocents isn't a god worth following," she retorted bitterly. "There were children at Cannes. What kind of god justifies the murder of babies?" Her voice broke as fat tears rolled down her cheek. "They said there was a group of twenty-two special needs teens from England at the festival tonight. They were all crushed as the wall fell. Twenty-two beautiful souls are gone just because some idiot thinks his god doesn't like rock music? It's insane!"

"Shhh. Georgia, stop crying, honey. You're killing me." Hick's voice was strained. "I agree it's insane. People like him are one of the reasons I do this, why I am who I am. They fuel the fire that keeps me going. We fight against them, fight for the innocents that died at the hands of this madman. We are the line in the sand that says 'no more.' We are the ones that protect the world from men like al-Bashir."

"I know you are. But I think about you going up against someone like him, and my stomach drops to the floor. You can't fight this kind of insanity. He's a special kind of crazy. People like that don't care. He'll do whatever he thinks he has to. Hick, what if you get hurt? What if..." she couldn't finish her thoughts and gulped instead.

"Honey," he soothed softly. "Shhh, it's ok. We're highly trained. When we go on missions, we've worked through every scenario. There are plans on top of plans. I trust my SEAL brothers completely as they trust me. You don't worry about me."

"I can't help but worry about you," she whispered. "Hick?"

"Yeah, honey?"

"I wish you were here."

"I wish I were there, too," he agreed. "It's just two more weeks. Hey, I was thinking, how about a little cabin in the mountains for a few days? We'll do some hiking, maybe a hot tub."

Annabeth snorted. "Hiking? Have you not seen me? The only hiking I do is the fourteen steps between my door and the condo's."

"Yes, Georgia, I have seen every beautiful curve of your delectable body and can't wait to have them in my hands again. Trust me to take care of you?"

The thought of his strong, callused hands caressing her body never failed to make an ache sit deep in her belly. She knew without a shadow of a doubt he would always take care of her. Her reply was breathy. "Yes, I trust you."

"Good girl."

She could hear the smile in his voice. She grabbed the remote and turned off the television. Right now, she needed him more than she needed to know what was going on outside her living room. She heard a ding as he turned the key and cranked his car. The fear was still in her mind, but she had pushed it back, focusing solely on him. Hick was 2,000 miles away, but he still made her feel safe. She thought about the conversation she and Ms. Clara had shared on the balcony. She had talked about Henry and how they had such a beautiful, full life together. She thought about her parents and the special love they shared. She wanted that. What's more, she wanted it with Hick. With every fiber of her being, she wanted a lifetime with him and to feel his warmth keeping her safe. At that moment she truly understood what Ms. Clara had meant. It was better to have one day with Hick in her life than an eternity without him.

"Hick?"

"Yeah, honey?"

"I need to tell you something."

"Let me pull off the road first. I don't want to wreck."

She half laughed. "It can wait. I don't want to keep you from going home."

His deep chuckle warmed her heart and made her toes curl. "You wait for me enough as it is. I can take a few more minutes before I get home. There, I'm safe. What do you need to tell me?"

She swallowed. Did she dare to do this now? On the phone?

"I... I..." she tried to get the words past her constricted throat. What if he bolted? Did she have the strength to keep going if he left her? Maybe it was better just to keep their relationship exactly as it was - uncomplicated. However, if she didn't tell him and something happened on one of his missions, could she live with knowing he never knew how she felt?

"Go on, spit it out."

She swallowed and steeled herself. "I know we said we decided to talk about what's going on between us when we were face to face, but watching this tonight made me realize what kind of people you handle on your job. I want you to know how I feel. You are my best friend, even more so than Jos. I couldn't take it if something happened to you. I think I'd just shrivel up into a little puddle of gunk."

"Georgia..."

"No, let me finish while I have the courage. You need to know that you aren't just a friend with benefits for me. You aren't just a fun time. Even with 2,000 miles between us, I feel you in my heart. I tried to push it all aside, but I can't do it anymore. Levi Salter, you are my Henry, my anchor in this world. I don't want you to go one more day, one more second without knowing the truth even if it means you leave. I love you."

The silence was deafening. Annabeth winced as she waited for him to say something as she simultaneously dreaded what he would say. Was he trying to form the words that would crush her heart and deaden her soul? Was he going to laugh at her declaration? Had she lost him for good?

"God, Georgia," his voice was tight. "You just had to beat me to the punch, didn't you?"

"W-w-what?"

The deep timbre of his voice sent goose bumps over her body. "Here I was trying to figure out the perfect setting, the perfect time, the perfect everything so I could tell you how I felt and here you went and one-upped me while I sat on the side of the highway. We started this journey as friends, and it's become so much more now. I don't have the words to explain how deeply I love you, but I do. You're my everything."

Then the tears came again. "Levi," she breathed into the mouthpiece. "Really?"

"Without a doubt," he replied.

She swallowed then asked the question that burned her soul. "What about the other women you've been dating?"

He sucked in a breath. "Yeah, about that. I haven't actually been dating. Toad was telling the truth. Since meeting you, there hasn't been anyone else - just you, Georgia. Only you."

CHAPTER 9

The rumble of large trucks echoed through the room. Standing, the man went to the window and watched Amir as he motioned for the new arrivals to back up to the storage room. The doors were flung wide, and crates and boxes were loaded into the back. Walking back to his desk, he gathered up his notes and stuffed them into his rucksack. It was time to move to the final staging area.

10 days

Commander Jonathan S. Dixon poured over his emails when a knock sounded on his door.

"Come in," he called out but never raised his eyes from the screen. The sound of a throat clearing pulled his attention. "What is it, Daniels?"

"You're needed immediately, Sir. There are

members of NSA, CIA and Homeland Security waiting in 162."

Dixon knew this was major. Normally, he wouldn't be called into a meeting with that many acronyms involved unless it was urgent. He stomach dropped as he feared for the worse. Standing, he grabbed his lid and motioned for the staff secretary to lead the way. Arriving at the meeting room, he walked in. The room was full of people in both civilian clothes and uniform. This was big. Taking an empty seat next to a pretty brunette, he waited for the shoe to drop.

Two more brass entered then the door closed and a man wearing a black suit and slicked back black hair stood. Approaching the front of the room he addressed them.

"I'm Christopher Feltzer of Homeland Security." He proceeded to introduce the remaining suits. When he was done, he took a deep breath and dove into the reason for the meeting.

"As most of you are aware, the attacks perpetrated in Cannes, and Novi Sad came at a complete surprise. There was no chatter that anything was coming. This has had every intel gathering office scrambling. Then two days ago, we got a break."

He pressed a button, and the room darkened as a

bright light focused up front. Pieces of conversation between two people in a virtual chat room flashed on the screen.

"One of our technicians found this bit of data while scouring for specific phrases. Once they were spotted, we were able to decipher the conversations between these two individuals. Ladies and gentlemen, we have a prospective target."

The briefing room was packed to the limit with more than twenty SEALs and a vast variety of support personnel. The two teams, Alpha and Bravo, sat in clusters, talking among themselves quietly about the meaning of this massive call-in. Every one of them hoped it was time to put the terrorist to bed finally. Permanently. Haafiz al-Bashir's face had been plastered on every news outlet in the world as he gloated over the massive destruction wrought in his name.

A shrill whistle pierced the low rumble of voices. "Listen up," a man's voice barked. Immediately, silence dropped in the room.

Dixon stepped to the front of the room and

glared over the assembled. A veteran of almost fifty years, he had seen his share of evil in this world on an up close and personal level. At five-eleven and two hundred, sixty pounds, he was still a force of reckoning. His steel blue eyes showed no emotion as he addressed the gathering.

"This man," he pointed to a large poster containing al-Bashir's face, "was elevated to the number one spot on the list. Haafiz al-Bashir, code name 'Fedora' has become our top priority. As you are aware, we formed two tactical strike teams designated Alpha and Bravo." He pointed to the two sides. "The sole purpose of these teams is to take out Fedora with extreme prejudice."

He's steely glance took in the room as he continued. "He's getting ready to strike again."

The room filled with angry murmurs. Dixon silenced them by holding his hand up.

"We have received intel for an impending attack. Barcelona Spain will host an artistic show ten days from now. The show will feature works by world-renown sculptor Yasmena Riviera. *La Ninfa Erotica* is a collection of twenty-three statues depicting young women in suggestive and somewhat sexual acts. Crowds are expected to be in the thousands for each of the three days. This venue fits the MO for Fedora's group perfectly. The state department contacted the Spanish government in hopes of postponing, but they refuse. Because of the bombings in Cannes and Novi Sad, security had already been tripled. Given the new intel, the Spanish army will have the place on tight lockdown."

Toad raised his hand. "I volunteer to go be eyes at the show. You know, for the sake of goodwill."

Bruiser slapped him in the back of the head as the room chuckled. "We can't let you out of the playpen for one minute."

Railroad leaned over and whispered, "Naked statues, not women, you numbskull."

Toad shrugged nonchalantly. "Po-tay-to, po-tah-to."

Bruiser growled, "Put it back in your pants and pay attention."

When the laughs died down, Dixon continued. However, there was a slight smile on his face. "The intel netted us a surprise. We have a viable location for Fedora, and we're going to take him out before he can put his plans for Barcelona into action."

Once again the room erupted in voices. When it settled, he continued.

"Alpha team will take the lead on this one. Bravo is in reserve. The DOD has green-lighted this op with the full support of the State Department. Here is the information we have." The screen on the wall lit up with a map containing several marks on it. "It's time to put together a plan and stop this maniac once and for all. Wheels up in sixteen hours and I want to have at least three scenarios ready by then."

CHAPTER 10

The small house they had commandeered sat low in a row of similar ones. The neighborhood was in a state of decay, but it guaranteed their privacy. None of the cell would dare to show their faces either way, but it was better to be safe than sorry.

9 days

"That last one was too easy, Hick. You're going to have to work a little harder to stump me. A cave, whisper, and snake were pretty obviously *Harry Potter and the Chamber of Secrets*. You know I'm an HP fanatic."

The deep, rich chuckle vibrated through Annabeth as she curled up on her sofa, smartphone in hand. "I thought I had you on that one, Georgia."

She shook her head and grinned at the screen. Next to being in person, Skype was an acceptable second. "I'm going to come up with a really good one. We've been at a stalemate now for two months."

"What was the bet this time?"

She chewed her lip as if she couldn't remember. "Wasn't it a month of movie tickets? No that was last time. Breakfast in bed for a week? I think that's it. I can't remember for sure. Let's see - the first round was pizza."

"Which you won," Hick agreed.

"Second was a Chocolate of the Month membership," she continued.

"Which you also won."

"Yes, but you got the third one. Did you ever go get your mani-pedi?"

He frowned. "I think you lost that one on purpose."

"Who, me?" She feigned indignation. "Never. You take that back, Levi Salter. I'd never lower myself to throwing a wager when my honor is on the line not to mention my memory of completely useless information."

He snorted, causing the screen to jiggle slightly. "Not all of that information is useless. If I'm ever on one of those television game shows, you are my lifeline. "

She laughed and leaned back against her pillow, propping her telephone on her chest. "Well, you did pick a pretty old movie. You can't expect me to know everything."

"Georgia, don't kid a kidder. I know you and your father used to watch old movies and John Wayne was his favorite actor. I mean, come on. An oil can, fire, devil, and fist? Even Elliot could figure that one was *Hellfighters*."

"I guess you just caught me on a bad day," she sighed dramatically but knew he wasn't buying it. The truth was, she wanted him to win that round. The sight of her big strong SEAL with his feet getting scrubbed by nail technicians was something she would gladly pay good money. "You never answered my question. Did you go to the salon? I even made it easy and picked one near your apartment."

He grumbled under his breath. "No, I haven't been yet, and I don't know if I ever will. Do you realize that's where a lot of wives for some of the other teams go? I'd never live it down if I'm caught with my feet soaking in fru-fru juice."

"I didn't think about that." Annabeth's brow

wrinkled. "I'd never want to cause you embarrassment. I just wanted to do something nice for you. I'll tell you what, next time you come out here I'll treat you to my favorite place. Nobody will know you there. I swear you will love it. There is nothing like having your feet pampered to make every bone in your body go liquid."

Hick frowned. "I don't know if it would be a good idea to subject anyone to touch my feet. All these years in combat boots have done a number on them. "

"Shhh. Just take it."

He chuckled at her. She watched him reach a finger out and stroke the screen. She could imagine his touch as he glided down her face. "God I miss you, Georgia."

"I miss you too." Her eyes closed as she thought of him, his hands, his lips and his... well, everything. Saying she missed him was a gross understatement. Since they had declared their true feelings for each other, it was like a floodgate had opened. The thought of being thousands of miles apart physically made her ache. "When do you leave?" she whispered as she opened her eyes.

Hick glanced up at the wall then back to the screen. "Soon."

She could see the worry etching into the lines on his face. She understood that his missions were hard and extremely dangerous, but there was something about this one. In the past, whenever he had left, it was as if he hadn't a care in the world. This time was different. There was tightness around his eyes that made him scowl. She longed to reach through the phone and gently smooth the frown that dented his brow. Even his chin was set in hard lines, and the dimples she so loved were missing. He was worried, much more than she had ever seen him before. But what could make her normally happy-go-lucky man take on such seriousness? In a flash, she knew. She didn't ask because he wouldn't confirm or deny her query. It was part of being in the SEALs - the constant unknowing. Confirmation or not, she knew what he couldn't tell her.

They were going after al-Bashir.

Carefully she locked away the overwhelming panic that threatened to choke her in its icy grip. The last thing he needed was to worry about her fear. Instead, she brought the screen closer and peered into it. "You will be careful, okay?"

The smile didn't reach his eyes. Instead, they seemed almost haunted. "Always." He tried to sound chipper, but to Annabeth, it was hollow.

"I need to leave. Go ahead and send me the next puzzle. I'll work on it when I can."

"Alright." Her answer was low and breathy. "I'll come up with a good one for you."

"I know you will." He inhaled deeply. "Georgia..."

"Stop," her voice grew hard. She knew without a single doubt; she did not want to hear him give her an 'if I don't make it' speech. Being so far away when he was safe was bad enough; she couldn't let doubt come into play. Not now, not when everything was finally going right. Painting a smile on her face, she took a teasing tone to lighten the mood. "You're coming back to me. We danced around each other for a year, and now that we're honest with each other, I'm not going to let you off the hook, bucko. I have plans for you and your crusty feet."

His laughter was loud over the speaker. "My heart and my feet are all yours, honey. I'll call you as soon as I get home. Stay beautiful."

"Stay badass," she answered. "I love you."

"Love you too, my sweet Georgia. I'll talk to you soon."

He touched the screen lightly with one finger then he was gone; the screen instantly blank. Annabeth dropped her cell to the sofa cushion and closed her eyes. Releasing the fear that she could now allow to run through her psyche, her heart thudded, pumping blood through her body. Her hands shook, and her chest tightened until she was afraid she couldn't take another breath. Hick and his team were going after inarguably the most terrifying man currently walking on the Earth, the man responsible for thousands of deaths including innocent men, women, and children. He killed in the name of radical fascisms. Death rode at his heels, nipping like a starved hound for food. Hatred, violence, and injustice were his companions. The thought of the man who held her world in his hands anywhere near that monster made her stomach pitch and roil. Biting back the bile as panic swam over her, her mind raced to find a way out of the hole she felt herself slipping. Her hand shook as she picked up the phone and called the only person who could give her some hope and a tiny bit of perspective.

"Jos? Hey, it's Annabeth. Is River there?"

CHAPTER 11

The man glared at the drunken idiot passed out on the porch. The men were not allowed any mind altering substance and that included alcohol. Pulling his pistol from his waistband, he pressed the silencer fitted barrel to the man's head and pulled the trigger. He wasn't happy about this. Amir should have a tighter fist on his men. Now they would need another driver.

8 days

Bravo stood in the cramped room, elbow to elbow along with the twelve members of the support team. Eyes were glued to the computer screens showing movement on the ground as glowing red and green shapes thanks to the three drones carrying thermal imaging cameras flying silently over the compound nestled in the hills of upper Iraq.

"Two minutes until breach," one of the men manning the console murmured.

Hick pressed in closer, leaning on the table strewn with maps, half-empty cups of horrible coffee and other instruments used to plan this attack. Rarely had he been on this side of an Op, watching as another team took out a target. He thought there would be more noise. Instead, the only sound in the room was the click of the keyboards and the soft hum of the two Black Hawks standing at ready on the pad outside.

Drakker, the man in charge of the team, lifted his fist, causing the others to stop instantly. He made a motion, and two of the team broke off from the others. He knew those were the snipers who would provide cover when needed.

"That'll be Diablo and Tig going to nest," Railroad whispered in confirmation.

"It's too quiet," Dude muttered. "Where are the tangos?"

"Four sentries on the corners," Railroad answered. "If Fedora is there, then there should be a lot more than that."

A general mumble rolled through the room as others agreed.

The team executed their roles as a well-oiled machine. Hick lifted his gaze to another computer screen with boxes containing the live feed from the tiny cameras mounted on each SEALs shoulder. The view was vivid green courtesy of the NVG units. He followed the action as Druid shadowed Drakker to the entry point designated in the plans.

On another screen, Lincoln pressed himself against a wall as Mastiff slid around and slapped a line of explosives to the door leading into the compound. Quietly they withdrew.

"Eyes on tango," whispered Diablo.

"Eyes on tango," replied Tig.

Hick's gaze returned to the larger picture provided by the satellite orbiting overhead. The picture was grainy thanks to the low light source, but it showed the four sentries on the compound's corner continued to pace slowly; their bodies were a bright white against the gray of their surroundings. He shook his head. Something was wrong; he felt it all the way down to his bones.

"What are we missing?" Wolf's brow wrinkled as he studied the scene. Beside him, Bruiser glared as well. Their unease was contagious, spreading to the rest of the combined team.

"Alpha, you are at a go," the mission coordinator spoke into his coms.

The breath in Hick's lungs froze. There was a flash of an explosion as the wall was breached. Overhead, the four sentries dropped two at a time as the snipers took them out. On the ground, the ten remaining members of Alpha poured through the hole and into the compound.

The view from the mini cams jostled as the SEALs made their way down a hallway and deeper into the building. At the end of the hall, a room opened up with several doors leading out. With a few quick signals, the team spread out into three teams with each taking a different exit.

Hick's eyes flew over the screen, watching the teams as they worked their way deeper into the structure.

"Clear."

"Clear."

"Clear."

"Nothing?" Cookie pressed his knuckles into the table as he leaned over it. "This makes no sense. Where is everyone?"

"Maybe they got spooked," Finch muttered.

"Alpha, we're sending in Fritz. Regroup in the main chamber."

"Roger, command."

Fritz, an eighty pound German Shepherd, walked alongside his handler, Diesel through the breach and down the hallway. Like the rest of the team, he had a micro camera as well, securely mounted on the side of his collar.

Diesel removed the leash from Fritz's collar and gave him the command to hunt. At once, Alpha pressed themselves back to the walls to give the dog room to work.

The view was dizzying as the dog ran down one corridor, taking time to smell along the way. With a sneeze, he whirled around and returned to the main room. When he reached the end of the second tunnel, he stopped, sat and stared at the wall.

"Command, we have a positive for a hidden room at the end of two."

Diesel hurried to the end of the tunnel, clasped the leash back on the dog and led him out. As before, Mastiff slapped a line of explosives to the wall and retreated. From his camera, Bravo witnessed the wall explode into a pile of rubble.

"Why have three hallways that dead end with only one room?"

"Maybe they are trying to throw us off?"

Toad shook his head. "I don't like this. Every hair on my neck is sticking straight out."

Two SEALs entered the room carefully.

"Clear."

Their search was interrupted by a yell. "TANGO TANGO TANGO," Tig's voice filled the com channel.

"INCOMING," Diablo's voice echoed.

The shout from the two snipers was loud in the room. Hick whipped his head back around to the satellite and widened his eyes in shock. All around the compound, unfriendlies materialized out of nowhere like ghosts.

"Sons of bitches dug in with thermo-covers so we couldn't see them," hissed the console operator.

"It's a trap!" Bruiser slammed his fist on the table. "Bastards laid a trap."

"Alpha, you have over twenty tangos coming in hard."

"Diablo's down." They could hear the staccato of gunfire with each gasped yell.

"Damn!" Abe growled.

"We're surrounded! They're coming out of the walls!" Drakker shouted. "There are tunnels everywhere!"

"Bravo!" the mission commander roared. "You're up!"

F-bombs filled the room as Bravo scrambled for their gear. The mission had turned into a Charlie Foxtrot of epic proportions. As Hick ran to the Black Hawk and jumped in, he hoped they would get there in time to save their friends. They were only six minutes by air from the compound, but at the rate, things had soured during the mission, that may be six minutes Alpha didn't have.

Annabeth's reading glasses made a soft thump as they landed on top of the thick piles of papers scattered across the oak desktop. Peering across the expanse, she glared at the smug grin on her client's face.

"Andrew, be reasonable. This contract for *The Obsession of Veed* is extremely generous. This will be your first movie. They are offering $5,000 option for two years. Most options begin at around $1,000. Remember, it just means they are renting your rights for two years."

"That's two years with no assurance that a movie will be made. And, while they are holding my creativity in their deathly grip, no-one else can pick it up. I don't want 'maybe.' I expect you to do better than a low budget television series. You certainly did much better for Joselyn Chambers."

Annabeth pressed her fingers tightly to the bridge of her nose and silently counted to ten. They had been beating the hell out of this dead horse for hours now. The throbbing pulse behind her eyes intensified every second this arrogant peacock sat in her office. Getting herself under control, she plastered a stiff smile on her lips and tried again.

"As I have mentioned numerous times, Joselyn Chambers's situation is highly unusual. It's not often a first-timer is picked up by a major studio with an option they green light. You also have to remember that your work is in horror where hers is suspense and drama. They are two completely different genres. It's all in what the studios are looking for at any given moment. Look at it this way, every day thousands of books are published. The fact that your book, among all those millions, was chosen for an option is amazing. Many authors would kill to be in your shoes."

Andrew lurched forward and slammed his fist on the desk, missing her glasses by inches. "I am not like those hacks," he snarled in a low voice. "They throw a few words into a file, call it literature and press the self-publish button. To call what they do art is to call a child's crayon work a masterpiece. It's beneath me. I hired you to do a job. You are failing. If you are incapable of fulfilling your part of our agreement, I'll have my lawyer speak to you concerning a breach of contract suit. Perhaps then, you will stop fawning over Joselyn Chambers and represent me as you promised."

"And as I told you if you feel so strongly about my inability to represent you adequately, then exercise your option and find someone who is more suited to your specific requirements." The grin he flashed made her shudder with revulsion. How had she ever thought of him as interesting?

"No, you will get me a better contract, or I'll sue you." As he finished, he spun on his heel and stormed out of her little office, slamming the door behind.

"Lord, save me from fools and pompous, second-rate divas," she mumbled. Crossing her arms over the contract, she laid her head down and closed her eyes. "I know they all can't be like Jos, but could I maybe get a few that are at least somewhat reasonable? This crap is for the birds."

The theme of *Murder She Wrote* rose from her cell beside. Lifting her head, Annabeth punched the button. "Hey, Jos, I was just thinking about you."

Joselyn's voice was high and breathy. "Annabeth, honey, are you alright?"

Annabeth frowned. "Ye-e-e-s," she drawled slowly. "Shouldn't I be?"

"Oh, God, you haven't seen the news yet, have you?"

A two-ton ball of ice settled into her stomach. "No, what's going on?" She opened her top drawer, searching for the tiny remote for her television sitting in the corner under a layer of dust. The last time it was used was when Elliot had spent a weekend with her several months ago. Her trembling fingers closed around the black rectangle. Drawing it out, she dropped it on the floor. Retrieving it, she felt her pulse racing in her veins.

"Is it Hick? Jos, what happened?"

"That snake in the grass, al-Bashir posted a video a couple of hours ago. In it, he claimed American forces attacked the private residence of one of a distant relative in Iraq killing several unarmed inhabitants. According to him, the family fought back and managed to kill several of the raiders before successfully repelling the rest."

Annabeth smacked the remote against her palm and furiously pressed the button. When it didn't turn the television on, she threw it in frustration, shattering it on the wall. "What else? I know you are hiding something from me."

Joselyn hesitated a few moments. "There were pictures; grainy ones like taken from afar. It showed a soldier slumped on a rooftop. A helicopter is burning on the ground. They claim they killed six and wounded many more."

"Oh my God," Annabeth whispered. The room became bright as if a 1000 watt light bulb suddenly flicked on. "I think I'm going to pass out."

"Put your head down. Try to stay calm. Maddox is on the phone trying to find out anything he can. He said he doubted this was true; it didn't follow what he knew about SEAL missions. Did you hear me, Annabeth? He said he didn't think it was true."

"What if it is?" Annabeth's hands were shaking badly, and goosebumps had broken out all over her body. "Jos, what if he's gone? We just figured out this thing between us. I don't think I can handle it if he's gone."

"Annabeth! Don't kill him off so quickly. Hick

and the other guys are all highly trained. Maddox says they have plans on top of plans. He said to try and not worry."

"Let me have the phone." Annabeth heard River's voice in the background. She gripped the chair arms as the sound of the receiver changing hands crackled in the speakers.

"Alright, I spoke to a friend, Tex. He can find out anything about anyone. He confirmed there was a fight and it was bad. I asked him about my team, and he said they are badly battered, but they made it out alright. Hick's alright. Did you hear me Annabeth? Tex says Hick is fine."

Annabeth heard, and the wave of relief that washed over her could drown an elephant. Hick was alright; battered, but alright. She didn't care what battered meant; she was just relieved he was still alive. Putting her head down next to the speaker, she swallowed. "Yeah, I hear you River," she whispered.

"I'm going to call Grace," Joselyn promised.

"No, don't. Kenseth is out of state, and she has Elliot. I'm okay. I'll wait until my nerves calm down then go home. I think I'm done for the day in the office."

"I'll stay on the phone with you."

"No, you go ahead. I'm fine."

"Are you sure?"

Annabeth thought about the news, the ups and downs of the last few minutes. Nodding absently, she whispered, "Yes, I'm alright. Thank River for checking for me."

"Honey, we wouldn't let you go through this alone. I'll tell him when he gets off the phone. He's calling Olivia to let her know. I'm sure she's going out of her mind worrying as well."

"We need a support group. I don't know how the other wives go through this."

Joselyn's voice turned bitter. "Maddox told me this is unusual. Normally, the guys are home long before any sort of news comes out. This jackass terrorist jerk couldn't wait to spin his propaganda."

"So basically, I won't know he's hurt until he's standing there with blood all over him?"

"Pretty much. At least then you can see with your own eyes that he's alive."

"Okay."

Annabeth stared at the words on Andrew's contract until they blurred and thick tears splattered the type. "I think I'm going to go home now. I'll wait for him to call me while I drown my sorrows in a tub of Death by Chocolate. Maybe whiskey. Hell, I may mix the two. Right now I think I need a dose of both."

"Alright, honey. Call me when you get home so I won't worry too."

"Okay."

When the phone disconnected, Annabeth lowered her head to her arms and let the flood go. Hick was alright. He was alive.

CHAPTER 12

The atmosphere was subdued in the ranks. Even with the victory yesterday, the coming event was heavy on everyone's mind. In less than a week, Allah would exact his revenge.

6 days

The rumble of the C-17 transport plane echoed in the cargo area. Bravo team along with the assorted equipment and supplies fought for space in the cramped hold. Along one side of the fuselage, the men rested, silently waiting for the signal that they had crossed back into American airspace. The ones who were still awake stared blankly ahead or down at their cell phones, anxiously awaiting the notification they could finally contact their loved ones.

Though technically, the mission had been a success, it had come at a great cost. When the dust cleared, all of the enemies were dead. However, Alpha team had taken a huge hit. Four of their fellow SEALs wouldn't be coming home this time.

"Diablo, Mastiff, Janitor and Razor," Finch muttered. "Four gone in the blink of an eye and seven injured including Diesel and Fritz."

"It was all a trap," Mozart growled. "They were waiting on us, dug in like ticks. You saw it happen. They waited until the team was in that tiny dead-end room before swarming them. The information was planted specifically to pull us in."

"Thank God Bravo was close, or it could have been a lot worse," Bruiser added as he readjusted his leg jutting out into the aisle.

"How's the leg?"

"Hurts like hell. Olivia is probably going to go apeshit when she sees it. I think it's worse for her because she's ex-army. She knows how fast things can fall apart." He ran a hand through his hair and leaned back.

"I can get Ice to talk to her if you think it'll help," Wolf volunteered. "She and the other women get together when we're gone. They're each other's support system."

"I may take you up on that."

"How about you, Hick? The shoulder doing alright? If you need to switch with me so you can rest your arm on the bags, it's okay with me."

"Stop mothering me, Finch. I'm fine. It was a clean shot on the top of my shoulder. Other than a little soreness, I don't even know it's there. It won't even slow me down." Hick snarled.

Finch threw up his hands in surrender. "Okay, Okay. I was just trying to be nice. Jesus."

"What's his problem," Abe asked.

"Which one," Railroad answered without opening his eyes. "Finch is overprotective, and Hick is worried what his *friend* is going to say when she finds out he's been shot." He made air quotes when he said the word friend.

"Leave her out of this," Hick bit out.

"Oh for God's sake, when are you going to man up and admit that Bethy is more than just a friend?" Toad jumped to his feet. The plane hit a pocket of turbulence causing them to sway precariously. Toad shot a hand out and braced against a stack of crates tightly webbed in against the floor. "Try another line because this bullshit you are shoveling isn't working."

Hick shot to his feet and shoved Toad roughly.

"You don't know what you're talking about. What happens between us is our business and nobody else's."

Toad smirked. "Well if there's nothing but friendship, maybe it's time she moved on. If you're not going to close the deal, I can do it for you. Redheads are tigers in the sack. Plus she's got all those curves... a man could spend a lot of time exploring."

Hick curled his hands into fists; his eyes narrowed as the veins in his temple pounded. "You lay one finger on Georgia I'll end you where you stand. This is your only warning."

Toad huffed. "That's another thing. Pick a damn name. Call her Annabeth or Georgia because I'm getting whiplash from her names and you saying you have a casual thing then getting all sentimental when you talk to her."

All eyes were open now and watching the shouting match between the two.

"What I call her is between us. The kind of relationship we have is too. You're the one spending all your time seeing how many girls you can bag. Jesus! Your freaking name is Toad because you hop from bed to bed!"

"Wow, I thought it was because he was their best swimmer," Cookie muttered to Benny.

"You know I don't tell people about my name," Toad snared and pulled his fist back as if intending on landing it on Hick's face. Suddenly, Wolf grabbed Toad as Bruiser pulled Hick back.

"Stop it, both of you. Sit down and cool off," Bruiser roared, twisting Hick around and pushing him into the seat. He hopped a step then bent over, groaning as a bright red spot bloomed on his thigh. "Great, I think the stitches popped."

Mozart rose up and grabbed a pack. "I'll take a look. Drop trou and take a seat."

The air was thick as soup from the tension radiating off Toad and Hick. The two glared at each other as Mozart unwrapped Bruiser's leg. "Yeah, you popped 'em," he grunted. Squatting down, he pulled supplies out of the med bag.

Hick flipped Toad a finger, turned to the side and propped against a stack of crates. The mutters of Mozart and Bruiser were lost in the noise of the hold.

"Look, we're all on edge here," Wolf finally piped up. "The mission was a Charlie Foxtrot. Just about everything that could go wrong did. Even with taking out Fedora's lieutenant, it feels like a failure because we lost brothers. The question now is how do we let this affect us? Do we break down and let them get in our heads or do we take this as a rallying call to take the bastard out once and for all? Right here, right now, we take the fight back to him. We don't let our loss become their motivation. You've seen the bullshit video he posted. He's gloating over this. I say we get our heads out of our asses and put the anger where it belongs - on him and not each other."

Toad blew out a breath. "I may have taken a tiny step over the line. Sorry, Bro."

Hick choked out a laugh. "Ya think?" Slowly the fury melted out of him. "Yeah, alright," he agreed. Facing Toad, he lifted his chin. "Me too. I'm just a little on edge about the mission, and then things with Annabeth have taken a turn. I haven't said anything because we're still trying to figure everything out. Either way, I shouldn't have let my temper get away from me."

"Yeah, me either," Toad returned.

"Are you going to kiss and make up now?" Benny asked flatly.

Everyone laughed. "If they do, I'm kicking their asses out of this plane without a chute," Railroad grumped then crossed his arms over his chest and closed his eyes. "We get enough of that lovey-dovey crap when Olivia and Bruiser are in the same room."

Mozart stood and glanced over at Benny. "How about you? Your side okay?"

"Yeah, just a scratch. I'm fine."

The big man nodded and gathered his supplies. Storing them in their bag, he returned to his seat and relaxed.

Static crackled from the speaker mounted on the ceiling overhead. "U.S. airspace," the pilot clipped.

Cell phones were dug out and turned on. Everyone had seen the propaganda released by al-Bashir and knew wives, girlfriends and family would be worried sick about them. Because of the engine noise vibrating through the space, privacy was at a premium. However, each man did as he could to damp the clatter somewhat.

Hick turned and cupped his hand around the mouthpiece of the phone. It only rang once before he heard the most beautiful voice in the world.

"Levi? Oh, thank God. Are you alright? I saw the video, and it about scared the life out of me. Where are you? Is everyone okay?"

He couldn't help but smile even though she was rambling. She was so damn cute. It didn't escape his notice that she had called him by his given name. She tended to do that when she was upset or worried.

"Slow down, Georgia. Yeah, I'm alright. We're a little beat up, but the team made it through."

"They said there were some casualties."

He blew out a breath. "We lost four brothers from another team."

"Oh my! I'm so sorry."

"Yeah, me too. "

"But you're alright?"

He heard the trepidation in her voice and hurried to reassure her. "Yes." He didn't like with-holding the truth from her, but he knew she would freak out right now. It would be better to wait until they were alone before he told her about his wound. He didn't want her upset when there was nothing he could do right now to calm her.

She obviously didn't buy it. Annabeth paused a few moments. "I want to Skype."

Hick blinked slowly. "Skype? Now? Right now? Why? I'm not home yet."

Her voice took on an exasperated tone. "Yes, now, so you can strip, and I can see for myself you aren't hurt."

He choked. Behind him, Hick heard someone snort. Turning his head, he saw Toad watching him. "You do it, I swear to God, I'm filming it and putting it on YouTube."

Ignoring him, he turned back to the conversation. "That wouldn't be a good idea, Georgia. The stripping part is definitely not a good idea right now."

"Is it because you're hiding something?"

"No, honey, it's because I'm on an airplane with ten guys who wouldn't appreciate me showing my Sunday best."

"You got that shit right!" Finch yelled out

Railroad joined in. "He strips, out he goes."

"Sorry. You'll have to take my word I'm okay."

Toad leaned in and shouted, "Yeah, besides the bullet hole isn't very big. He's had worse."

"Bullet hole? You got shot?" Annabeth screeched.

Putting his hand over his mouthpiece, he glared at Toad. "Thanks a lot, brother."

"Anytime," he smirked then winked. Dropping back into his seat, Toad pulled out his cell and began playing a game.

Hick considered a little lie but knew eventually she would see the wound. Bracing himself, he nodded absently. "Yeah, I got shot." He hurried to pacify her. "But it's a small place on the top of my shoulder. It's just a flesh wound. Doc checked it out and said I'll be fine. I'm not even going to get any recovery time off. Look, if you need to Skype to see for yourself, I can do that, but I'm not stripping. I'll save that for when we are alone."

"Hick," she breathed softly.

He could hear the hitch in her voice and knew she was close to tears. "Hey, hey, hey. It's ok, honey, I promise you. I told you I was coming home to you and I meant it. The Phoenix thing is this weekend. Think about it - just a few days and I'll be there. Okay?"

"Yeah, okay," she agreed reluctantly. "That cabin you're getting for us better have room service because we're not leaving until they have to come looking for us."

"If it doesn't I'll make sure to have it stocked for us. We won't have to leave. That okay?"

"Perfect."

"Alright, honey, I'm going to go now. I just wanted you to know I was okay and that I was thinking about you. I'll talk to you tonight."

"Okay. I love you."

"Me too."

He disconnected the call and slid his cell into one of the pockets of his BDU. Just talking to Georgia was enough to bring him out of his funk.

"Yep, you're right," Toad called out from his seat.

"I'm right about what?"

"Your relationship has changed."

"You're just jealous."

Toad lifted his shoulders in a shrug. "Maybe."

Hick frowned. That didn't sound like Toad. He was the carefree one. Was he thinking about finally shedding those wandering shoes?

"You okay?" Hick asked.

In reply, Toad grunted and kept his eyes on his game.

CHAPTER 13

The Maker arrived and went straight to work. Each device had a specific purpose and must be created according to rigorous specifications. The process will take several hours to complete. A last-minute addition to the order had the Maker frowning. The kill switch was imperative and would be added in at a hefty premium. Like most western jackals, money spoke loudly. Their greed overshadowed everything.

27 hours

"In conclusion, I know this is the first time for many of you to attend a convention of this size, and you are understandably nervous. However, please remember the other authors and artists behind those doors downstairs are all people too. They had their first attendance once. They sat in those same chairs and felt the giant goose sized butterflies in their stomachs. They survived, and you will survive too. You all have your packets of information that includes the table charts and event lists. Nothing is mandatory, just go when you want, if you want, but I encourage you to network as much as possible. This is an awesome opportunity for you to meet not only your peers but also cover artists, models, publishers, editors and an assortment of other professionals who can help you on your way. Just stay away from the artist's relations people. I need to pay my bills. Are there any questions?"

Annabeth's eyes twinkled mischievously as she added the last part. In reward, several of the seven authors she currently represented in the classroom chuckled. In the back corner, Andrew Stinger rolled his eyes and stood to his feet. Turning abruptly, he disappeared out the door. She frowned. Well, that was true about all of her clients except for him. Even though she believed in his work as she did all her clients, she would be more than happy to see him wander off to another agent. His mood swings were getting on her nerves. Maybe it was the disastrous date they had gone on. Up until that point, he had been charming, but the appeal was over. The prince had turned into a frog. Either way, she wouldn't be sad to see him go.

"Alright then. Thank you all for trusting me to be your representative and remember there will be a reception Monday evening. The information is in the packet you have. Everyone have a great time, and you have my number on speed dial. I'm here to help you. However I can."

Everyone stood and started to make their way toward the door. Annabeth picked up her satchel and purse, took a big breath and pasted a smile on her face. *Here we go, old girl, let's get this show on the road.*

"Annabeth!"

She whirled around and came face to face with Joselyn. With a squeal, she threw her hands out dropped her bags and hugged her friend tightly. "Jos! I saw you sneak in during the talk. You've been through my spiel before; you didn't have to come."

Joselyn let her friend go and stepped back. "Of course I had to come. You've been there with me every step of my career with your support, how could I ever do less?"

In response, Annabeth smiled and took a step back. "Pffft. As if you could ever be a burden. I would love to have another dozen clients like you." She peeked over Jos's shoulder and grinned. "Hey River. You're looking as hunky as always. Are you ready to hit a few covers yet? I can get you a contract just like that." She grinned as she snapped her fingers. "I like the beard. The silver fox is very 'in' right now. The ladies love that distinguished, sexy, mature look."

It was an old joke between them. Joselyn's husband was an ex-SEAL and one of Hick's former team members. Like the rest of them, he was buff and beautiful - if one could call a badass alpha male beautiful. The first time they had met, she had tried, unsuccessfully, to get him a contract with one of her model representative friends. As always, he laughed then pulled her into his arms for a warm hug. "Nope, sorry, I don't have time for lying around and eating bonbons."

The hug ended, and she took a step back. "Oh, yeah, the breeding thing you and your cousin are doing. It must be doing well."

He grinned and bobbled his head in a non-comitial manner. "Shaun and I are doing well. After my uncle had to give up his program years ago on the farm, he thought he couldn't get it back. We've got it off the ground now. We even got a new bull that has an excellent pedigree. It's only been a year so we have a ways to go before we can see a difference in the cattle and expect our profit margin to increase. But *that* breeding program is not what's keeping me busy." He emphasized the word 'that' as he wrapped an arm around Joselyn and gently splayed a hand over her midsection. Looking at Annabeth, he waggled his eyebrows suggestively. Jos placed her hand over his and looked over her shoulder, smiling gently as her eyes filled with tears.

Annabeth's hand flew to her mouth. "Oh my God. Are you? I mean she? You? Oh my God!" Annabeth squealed and grabbed them both and hugged tightly. "I'm going to be an Aunt?"

Jos nodded as she wrapped her arms around her best friend. "Not only an Aunt but also a godmother. If you are willing?"

Annabeth felt her throat clamp up. Swallowing back the tears she looked at the two and nodded. "I couldn't be more honored." Wiping her face, she took a deep breath. "Congratulations, you two. I'm so happy for you both. How far along are you?"

"Just thirteen weeks. We wanted to wait to tell everyone until I was a little further on. You're the first we told outside of our parents. I swear his mother already has a nursery built."

"We'll this sells it. I've been thinking about getting a new car. Mine is over ten years old and good for local stuff. But, if I'm going to be burning up the miles between Atlanta and Mississippi, I'll need a new one."

Joselyn laughed. "You'll have plenty of time to go shopping. He or she has a long time to bake yet. How is everything else?"

"It's going well. I've picked up a part-time apprentice, Oscar. Nice kid, young, eager to learn the ropes but a little high strung. I'm trying to calm him down a bit. I told him if he didn't learn how to chill, he was going to have a heart attack before he hit twenty-five. He wanted to come this time, but he's a senior in college and taking summer classes so he can walk next June. I told him to study, get good grades and if he still wanted to be in this business after hanging out with me a year, I'd pay for him to go to next year's convention in Seattle."

"You're a good woman, Annabeth Switcher."

Annabeth smiled. "So are you, Joselyn Benson."

"I don't see Hick. I figured with you being only a few hours from California; he'd be here." River looked around the almost empty room.

Annabeth's face fell. "He's not going to make this trip, but we're planning some time next weekend. I'm taking a few days off. With everything that's been going on lately, he's had to stay close to home. Plus, tomorrow morning is the memorial service for the SEALs that died. I wish I could be there for him."

"I'm sure he knows, honey," Joselyn murmured as she squeezed Annabeth's arm. "I told Maddox he should go. They are like brothers."

"My place is here with you." River slid his arm around her waist and pulled her against him. "Uncle Sam and the team had me for twenty years. Now you and the sprout need me. The guys would understand that. It doesn't mean I care any less for them. Hell, Diablo and I went through sniper training together. But he'd be the first one to tell me to stay here." He nuzzled her neck tenderly. "I couldn't leave you now if I tried. There's no way I'm letting you out of my sight until the baby is born and maybe not even then."

Annabeth's cell chimed, and she pulled it out of her pocket. Andrew Stinger's name flashed on the screen. With an exasperated sigh, she lifted it up. "I need to take this. I'll see you guys on the floor."

As the two turned to leave the room, Annabeth took a deep breath and forced a pleasant tone. "Hi, Andrew."

"This table will not do. The space is too small. I specifically told you I wanted to be against a wall.

I'm going to get paranoid with all the people walking around behind me."

Annabeth rolled her eyes and gritted her teeth. "I'll be right there," she calmly replied as she gathered up her things. Disconnecting the call, she dropped her cell into her pocket and rubbed her already aching head. Normally, conventions were one of the things she loved the most about her career. She enjoyed networking with other professionals, meeting new potential clients and watching her current ones experience meeting their fans. Normally it was a tiring but rewarding experience.

Then there was Andrew Stinger.

She sighed as she pushed through the door of the small meeting room she had booked for the orientation talk she always gave her clients before a big convention. Because of him, the next four days were going to last forever. But after that, God willing, she would get several days with Hick, and that would be worth it.

CHAPTER 14

The men assembled in the small backyard, dressed in identical black clothing. The man watched as Amir inspected each one carefully including their weapons and extra rounds. He could feel the thrum of excitement running through the cell as they were given the last commands including the one to load the truck.

5 hours

The early morning memorial service had finished. Still, in their dress white uniforms, Bruiser and his team gathered at his house. It was new, and even though Olivia had several candles burning, the smell of sawdust and paint laid heavily underneath. The couple announced yesterday that several weeks ago they had eloped to Las Vegas. Bruise had no family, so they had taken Olivia's brother and aunt with them. Toad assured the team, the eventual reception thrown by the SEAL team would be of epic proportions.

Even with Bruiser's good news, the mood in the room was somber. Saying goodbye to four brothers had been difficult, and each of them felt the loss deep in their souls. Even though they hadn't worked too closely together, SEALs were still a family, and they mourned the death of their brothers.

"I'm surprised the Navy gave us seventy-two hours leave. I figured they would have us back on Fedora's trail first thing." Railroad took another drink of his soda.

Bruiser tightened his grip on Olivia sitting next to him with her head leaning on his shoulder. She had her eyes closed and appeared to be sleeping. "We'll need to have our heads in the game," he said as his thumb made slow, lazy circles on her arm. His eyes wandered over her face. It was easy to see how much he loved her. She opened hers and looked longingly into his.

Hick was reminded of Annabeth and the hundreds of miles currently between them. What he wouldn't give to be able to hold her, touch her and just be with her right now. He shook off the thought.

It would drive him crazy if he let it. Instead, he turned away and lifted his chin at Cowboy. "How's your dad? Are you back home for good?"

His friend sighed heavily and shook his head. "I'm only here for the service and to take care of a few things before going back to Wyoming. They finally found a chemotherapy that is shrinking the tumors, but it also knocks Dad down hard. He's got another two rounds, and then they'll discuss surgery. The only way to get rid of it completely is to remove his leg. Dad has always been a strong man intent on doing everything himself. It's hard to let us kids take care of things. The Navy gave me six weeks emergency family leave which should take me through his surgery. Afterwards, I'll be back."

"We've missed you."

"Aww, Toad, I didn't know you cared," Cowboy puckered his lips and made a kissing sound.

"Damn right we do. There's nobody to save us from Hick's cooking while you're gone."

Hick frowned. "I haven't cooked, Toad."

"And if you had, nobody would have saved us."

A chuckle filled the room then died away as the others talked among themselves. Hick walked to the back door and out onto the small deck. Leaning on the railing, he turned his face to the sky. It was a beautiful day with the sun shining and the sounds of happy people everywhere. It felt wrong, somehow. Where was the justice in a gorgeous day when they had said goodbye to four brothers who gave everything to keep this country and every inhabitant safe? He drew in a deep breath and let it out slowly, turning his mind from the maudlin thoughts. The air was filled with the scent of the ocean. Even though he had lived here for years, it still felt unnatural to him. California was his home but sometimes he didn't feel it. Right now, he felt a little homesick. The problem was it wasn't Boston he was longing for, but rather Annabeth. His fingers itched to touch her cream speckled skin. His heart ached to see her smile. Instead of the salty sea air, he wanted to wrap himself in her scent and drown.

"You okay?"

Hick whirled around. "Yeah, hey, Toad, I'm fine. I'm just thinking about things."

"Things like Annabeth? I saw how you watched Bruise and Livy. It was almost envious."

"I do envy them." He blew out a breath and gathered his thoughts. "I know Livy is still recovering from her ordeal and Bruiser is beside himself worrying. But at least they are together. It's killing me being so far away from Georgia. Whoever said long distance relationships sucked wasn't just whistling Dixie. It sucks big time."

"Then do something about it."

Hick threw his hands up. "What? What can I do? It's not like I can ask for a transfer to Atlanta. It's either here or Virginia Beach. Those are the only two options available for SEALs. I mean, Virginia Beach would be closer, but you guys are here. I'm a part of this team, and it's where I belong."

"Simple, move her here. You said yourself that her job is not static. She can do her thing anywhere." Toad beamed at his obvious solution. "Easy peasy, gotta squeeze me."

Hick laughed. "I don't think that's how the saying goes. Besides, her family is there. Her history and everything she has is there. I can't ask her to give that up."

"Have you?"

Hick's eyebrows wrinkled in confusion. "Have I what?"

Toad huffed. "Have you asked her to give it up?"

"Jesus, Toad, of course not. It's not fair of me to do that."

"But you two hurting from the distance between you, that's fair?"

"Hush it. You don't know what you're talking

about," Hick growled. "What Annabeth and I have is something strong. It's a special attachment. When you care about someone, you don't make demands on them."

His friend choked out a laugh. "You think just because the girls I date are one-night-stands, I don't understand what it feels like to have a connection to someone?" He moved over and leaned against the railing beside his friend. "I know what it means to connect to a special person. I understand it a hell of a lot more than any of you guys ever knew." He picked at a splinter on the rail, pulling at it until he ripped a long thin sliver of wood away. Using it, Toad poked at a splat of bird droppings resting between them. "Did you know I had a sister?"

Hick startled. "No. I thought you were an only child. I remember you saying you were an only child."

"I am. Now." He studied the splat intently a few moments before continuing. "Rayna wasn't just a sister; she was my twin."

"What happened?"

"She died."

"Ah, jeez, man. I'm sorry."

Toad lifted his shoulders in a shrug. "It is what it is. Things that we experienced shape who we become. I'd like to say I've gotten over it, but I haven't. I never will and to be honest I don't want to. Losing her was losing a piece of my soul. To get over it, that would be like forgetting her."

"You don't have to talk about it," Hick told him mindful of the pain radiating off his friend.

"I want to." He shook his head. "No, I don't want to, but I think I need to. It's time."

The two stared out over the yard as the wind meandered through the tall palms and shrub making a soft sighing sound. Somewhere, down the block, a set of wind chimes sang softly. It was tranquil and cathartic, and neither man said anything for a while. Finally, Toad cleared his throat.

"Growing up, I was the one that always got into trouble. I was the class clown. She was the nerd. I would spend time in the principal's office, and she'd be in the library. I did sports; she did debate and chess. You couldn't get any more different between us if you tried."

He tossed the sliver and turned back to stare at the house." Even though we were opposites, we were always close. Sharing a womb will do that, or so they say. 'You are so brave, Reese,' she would say. 'I wish I was more like you.' I'd do anything for her. She had me so wrapped around her pinky, I couldn't breathe, and I was happy to be there. Nobody messed with her because everyone knew she was Reese Harkin's sister and I didn't give a shit if it was a guy or a girl, adult or teen, you screwed with Rayna, and I'd bring hell on your head like it was Armageddon. I was very protective of her. To the extreme at times. The first week of high school, a senior pushed her down some steps. She nearly broke her ankle. She told me what happened and the next day, I found him bragging to his cronies about it. He thought it was funny so I showed him how much fun a broken ankle could be. I got my ass handed to me by the three of them but I made my point. Didn't regret it then, don't regret it now. The only reason I didn't get expelled was he didn't rat me out. Come to find out, his dad was a bigger bully, and if he found out a freshman had whipped his son, he would get twice as much at home. He insisted it was an accident even with witnesses saying different. The best part of it, afterward, everyone stayed clear of me and her."

Toad braced his hands on the railing and leaned back, lifting his gaze to the cobalt blue sky above.

"Rayna wanted to live a little more, explore a bit. So, I tried to give her those opportunities. When we graduated, we were going to be going separate ways. She got a full ride to Rice. I was going to Clemson on an athletic scholarship. It was going to be the first time in our lives that we weren't living in the same city, much less the same part of the country. I thought this would be an opportunity for her to get a little fun under her belt, so I talked her into going to a party. I wanted her to see a little of the world around her before she immersed herself in school without me there to make sure she was alright. That was such a mistake."

Hick put his hand on Toad's shoulder, silently lending him strength. Toad took a few cleansing breaths and continued. "She hadn't ever had alcohol before, and it went straight to her head. She started dancing on a table with some other girls, and before I could get through the crowd to get her off of it, the table fell, tossing her over the side of the balcony. She hit the concrete head first. Three weeks in the ICU and she never woke up. My parents had to decide to turn off the life support."

"Damn, Toad, I'm sorry. I didn't know."

He shrugged. "Nobody knows. Not even Bruiser. It's not like that's a conversation you have with your friends. 'Hey, let's have another round at the bar. By the way, my twin sister died when I was a kid. Pass the pretzels.'" Toad's tone was tight.

"And you didn't go to Clemson but joined the Navy?"

"The day after her funeral, I enlisted, and I haven't been home since. My parents blame me for her death, and they're right. It's all my fault."

"No, it's not your fault. It's a stupid accident. They're hurting just like you."

"Maybe. But since then, I don't form relationships. They just don't work for me. Why work for a relationship when they never last? My sister had been there with me every moment of my life until suddenly she wasn't. Nobody could ever be that close to me again. When she died, my family died. Nothing can replace that, and I don't even try."

Hick understood now. Toad was the way he was to keep from feeling anything real for someone else. He emotionally cut himself off from others to protect himself. It was his defense because in his eyes, people you cared for left. His sister, his family, the people that should always be there for him was gone, leaving him with nothing. He couldn't blame him.

"Hey, I know this hurt you, but it's no reason to lock out the possibility of something with someone else. There are good people out there. You deserve to be happy, too, Toad. Let someone in every once in a while."

"Stop analyzing me. I'm fine. I'm happy just like I am. I have the team and my career. It's more than enough. You and Bruiser can have your relationships. That's what makes you happy. Me, I enjoy the freedom of being perpetually detached."

"It sounds painful."

"Says the man pining over a woman living on the other side of the country."

"Touché."

The two stood in silence, listening to the sounds of people around them. Inside, one of their team members laughed at a joke.

"I got an idea."

Hick raised an eyebrow. "I'm afraid to ask."

"No, this is a good idea. We've got three days leave. How about we take off for Phoenix and spend them there."

Hick almost got whiplash from the 180 Toad had just thrown. "She's working."

Toad snorted. "She's got to sleep sometime. She'll need to eat and don't you think it would be nice to spend what time you can with her? You were just bitching about not seeing her enough."

"True." Hick thought about it a minute. "It would

be nice to spend whatever time I can with her. But why would you want to go?"

"Two reasons. First, it's a five-hour drive, but I can get us there in three and a half. Second, did you know there will be models there? I've been checking up on those conventions. Have you seen the women for some of those book covers? Big eyes, big lips, big...." He cupped his hands before his chest.

"Everything," Hick finished for him.

Toad laughed. "Yeah, everything. It's a smorgasbord, and I'm feeling a little peckish. Three days of all-you-can-eat beauties sound like a trip to heaven to me." He glanced at Hick's face full of indecision. "Let me put it this way; I'm going with or without you."

"Oh, in that case, yeah. Someone has to save the women of Phoenix from you."

"Nah, brother," he slapped Hick on the shoulder causing him to rock. "The ladies are in for a treat. They get one look at me, and I'll be the one needing saving."

CHAPTER 15

The man hopped off the truck, not watching them as they continued down the road. Quickly, he walked down the street and to the next block. Reaching his destination, he strolled into the hotel and received a key for a room on the top floor facing the Sadder Center. He shook his head when asked about luggage then ignored the elevator and climbed the stairs. The room had been chosen specifically for the view. He checked his camera and prepared to record. Today would be a glorious day, and he would document it for The Left Hand.

The entire world will watch their glorious victory.

1 hour

The North American Literary Exposition was the single biggest convention of the year. With more than 1200 exhibits, vendors, and artists, it represented a vast diversity of everything bookish. Annabeth worked diligently to get her clients involved each year, and within weeks of the close of this year's, she would begin to work on the next one. Looking over the huge floor on the lower level of the exhibition center, she felt that familiar tingle in her belly. This was her time to shine, and she was more than ready for the challenge.

The majority of the authors were still busy in the top two floors doing their seminars, roundtables and visiting the vendor's showcase in the upper ballroom. That left only a few hundred scattered on the main floor. She knew that number would swell exponentially in the next couple of hours when the public meet and greet flung its doors wide and welcomed in the populace already gathering outside. More than ten thousand people were expected to flow through the four-day event before it was over.

Pulling out her table chart, she noted the booths marked on the page. Her clients were spread out all over the floor. Glancing at the fitness monitor on her arm, she grinned. She would get her steps in today, no doubt.

Forty minutes later, she had worked her way

around the right side. Andrew's table was next, but she was not looking forward to seeing him. It had taken her most of an hour last night to calm him down and "fix" the problems he had with his booth. She pointed out that he was actually in an optimum location as he had a straight view of the front entrance where readers and fans could see him immediately. When he complained about being in the open, she pointed out that the tables were set and if he moved now, his fans wouldn't know where to find him. She then talked to the lady who sat to his back and arranged to have their standing banners placed so that they had a wall of sorts between them. He was pacified. For the moment.

Arriving at his booth, she let out a breath of pure relief to find it empty. Andrew must be at one of the events or perhaps in the bathroom. Taking out one of her cards, she scribbled a quick note on the back and left it for him.

Andrew - I stopped by to check on you. Your booth looks wonderful! I'll be back later after seeing my other clients. Call me if you need anything. - A

Dropping it onto his chair, she turned and hurried to the next one on the list just as her cell rang. Seeing it was Joselyn, she stopped mid-aisle and answered.

"Jos! I'm working my way back to you. It'll be a few minutes. Everything alright?"

"Could you come now? There's something you need to see."

She wrinkled her brow. "Sure. I'll be there faster than a toupee in a hurricane."

Dropping her cell into her bag, she made a sharp left and headed out of horror and into the area reserved for romantic suspense. This was the first year of grouping genres, and Annabeth thought the change would be a good one. She had been harping at the committee about it for years.

When she found Joselyn, she frowned and made it a point not to let Andrew know where she was. Joselyn had a fantastic spot against the wall in the bottom of the T and less than thirty feet from the hallway leading to the bathroom. Already her posters and banners filled the large double booth as River moved one of the boxes containing her books to rest against the wall. Huffing, Annabeth stopped and leaned on the table. Blowing a strand of her hair out of her face, she asked, "Alright, I hurried my little-dimpled hiney right over here. What's the problem? Do you need some help? "

Jos looked up from where she was stacking cover cards and arranging pens. The black covered table was stacked with assorted swag she would be giving away. Annabeth picked up a bright green piece of candy and unwrapped it. Popping it into her mouth, she grinned. "Damn I love these Happy Orchard candies."

"Maddox always makes sure I have a bowl full at these events. I told him I have no self-control with those and they go straight to my hips."

River bent down and kissed his wife tenderly. "You're binging for two now. Enjoy your sweets, honey. I love you and your hips, no matter how huge they get. Besides, I know how to whittle them down if you need to, though I think our daily exercise program keeps you in great shape."

Joselyn's face exploded in red as her husband wiggled his eyebrows suggestively. She smacked him in the arm. "Behave. Annabeth doesn't want to hear your pervy thoughts concerning our sex life."

Annabeth nodded. "Yeah, no, you can keep that to yourself. I love you guys, but that is on the 'oh hell no' list. Now, you had a problem?" She raised one eyebrow at her friend. "Aside from the obvious one smirking behind you like a jackass eating briars? What can I help you with?"

"Oh yes, sorry. I got distracted. The problem is I

have too much help. I'm hoping you can fix that for me." Joselyn waved a hand to her left.

As she turned, Annabeth's eyes widened when a tall, muscular man stepped out of the bathroom hallway. Grinning at her, Hick waggled his eyebrows and leaned against the door frame with his hands stuffed into his pants pockets. He was wearing a light yellow, short sleeved button up that showed off his well-defined arms and the sculpted definition of his pecs where the top three buttons were undone. The tails hung over the waist of his medium wash jeans that hugged his muscular thighs and ended with a pair of loafers. In appreciation, Annabeth's eyes traveled up his frame as she licked her lips unconsciously. Dear God, that man was sextacular to the infinity power.

"Georgia... my sweet Georgia... no peace will I find. Just my memory of you keeps my Georgia on my mind."

His voice was deep and rich as he sang his version of the song that always made her heart melt. Her feet were rooted to the spot as she listened to him serenade her and then she was running, kicking out of the low heels she had worn today as a smattering of applause erupted around them. He caught her easily as she wrapped her arms around his neck and pulled him down for a kiss. At that moment, all the doubt, the fear, and the loneliness disappeared along with the room as he cradled her head tenderly. He drank from her lips, thirsty for her as a man lost in the desert. His grip was firm, holding her securely, telling her she was precious to him. She pressed herself against him tightly, clinging to him as his lips and tongue dismissed the distance that had been between them for far too long.

"Georgia, Georgia. My beautiful, fiery minx," he whispered against her lips then nipped the bottom gently, sucking it into his.

She whimpered softly, clawing at him. "Hick," she sighed breathlessly. Her body ached for him. She knew she couldn't tear the clothes from him and drink in every delicious inch of his toned body, but she couldn't for the life of her remember why at the moment. Her eyes met his half-lidded ones, and she saw the inferno burning there for her.

"Ahem," a masculine voice sounded behind her. "You two need to get a room," Toad grumbled.

Oh yes. That was the reason she couldn't have her wicked way with him. They were undoubtedly putting on quite the show. Reluctantly, she untangled her fingers from his hair and took a hesitant step back. His arm shot out and wrapped around her waist pulling her to fit against his side as if she belonged there. She grinned. Well she did, didn't she?

"Oh my Lord, that was hot," a woman said to Annabeth's right. She glanced over and saw one of the authors fanning herself with a stack of cover cards. Beside her, another woman nodded in agreement.

"I'm making notes. My next hero is going to sing to my heroine. That's so freaking hot and sweet my panties just melted right off."

Annabeth's face turned a bright red. Then her eye widened at Toad strolled over and threw his hand out. "Ladies, I'm Reese. I'd be honored to help you with those pesky panties."'

"Oh my God," Joselyn exclaimed and turned away. Looking up at her husband, she asked, "Can't you do something about him?"

River laughed and shook his head. "Honey, we've been trying to rein that one in since the first day he walked in the door. Hick brought him; it'll be his duty to wrangle him."

Hick drew his arm tighter around Annabeth and shook his head. "Nah, I've got my hands full." He looked down into her eyes and touched her cheek gently just as he did when they Skyped. "They are very full."

The tender reunion was shattered as a loud boom echoed through the 200,000 square foot exhibition hall. Everywhere, banners flipped over and stacks of books collapsed. Screams followed by shouts filled the space. Annabeth looked around in a panic, trying to ascertain from where the noises originated. All the way across the floor a cloud of smoke enveloped the air, reaching out towards the back with bilious phantom fingers.

"What the hell? Is that a truck?" Hick peered into the advancing gloom.

River helped Joselyn to her feet then shot a look toward the front of the hall. "I can't tell."

"Yeah, it's one of those cargo ones. It looks like someone was backing up and ran into the front of the building. Half the wall has collapsed. I'll go see if anyone is hurt," Toad replied as he started to jog toward the wreck.

"Honey, stay here while I..." Hick had pulled away from her when the doors on the panel truck opened and a mass of men dressed in black carrying weapons flowed out. They swept along the walls, pushing tables back and overturning chairs as they herded people toward the middle. A smaller group of men unloaded large boxes from the truck. When they were finished, one of them slapped something onto the side of the truck where it met the partially collapsed wall and ran. A heartbeat later, a monstrous explosion rocked the building, throwing them to the floor. Annabeth pushed up on her hands and glared toward the front. Where the truck had been lodged, there was now a pile of rubble and glass along with blackened, twisted metal that smoldered and set off the sprinkler system. Her ears rang so loudly she couldn't hear anything else. She knew people must be screaming as they got up and ran toward the exits with their mouths open. She turned her head just as one of the doors were flung open, and a figure dressed all in black including black boots and a black ski mask stepped through. He carried a large rifle of some sort which he pointed up toward the ceiling. He shouted something then began to fire over the heads of the people surging toward him. Annabeth stuck her fingers in her ears, reamed them around a moment then pulled them out, hoping to restore her hearing. She turned a panicked face toward Hick as he gathered her in his arms protectively. What was going on here?

More of the doors were flung open and more strangers entered the hall. Hick pulled her out of the way, back to where Joselyn and River were. She saw Joselyn peeking out from behind one of the large banners at the rear of her table. River stood in front of it, his eyes on the melee happening in the room. Hick pushed her gently to their table, and around the side. Without saying a word, he lifted his chin toward the banner. She understood in a heartbeat. He wanted her to join Joselyn in hiding. Reluctantly letting his fingers go, she willed her frozen feet to move and slid into the tiny space between banner and wall. Joselyn's face was white as she reached out to grasp her friend's trembling hand.

Her hearing slowly returned, and she could pick out the sounds of people sobbing and screaming mixed with the annoying clang of the fire alarm. The room quieted suddenly as the alarm stopped and the sprinkler system gave one last spurt before joining it in silent death.

"Hick?" she whispered.

"Shh, baby. Stay still and quiet," he mumbled. "Try not to be scared."

Ha! As if that was humanly possible. She wasn't just scared; she was completely terrified. Her knees knocked so hard, it was amazing they weren't found immediately. Stifling a whimper, she glanced at Joselyn and saw the same horrified fear mirrored on her face as well.

There were several bangs then sounds she

couldn't place. Peeking out the side, she saw a team of three men carting in a large crate followed by another one carrying a thick chain. The door slammed, and he wrapped the chain around the handles and locked it with a padlock.

"Damn. They're sealing the exits, "River muttered."Where's Toad?"

"He slipped out just before the explosion."

Son of a bitch.

As soon as Toad realized what was going on, he got Hick's attention and signaled he was going for help. He knew his friends would never leave their women alone so that left him to find assistance. First thing was getting to a safe place and figure out the best course of action

Toad eased along the corridor, past the bathrooms to a small utility door at the end. He heard voices coming his way so tugged on the door only to find it firmly locked. Pulling out the Swiss Army knife Rayna had given him on their last Christmas, he used the tool to jimmy the lock. It was worn and pretty useless for much of anything, but he kept it with him as a memento of her and for luck. When the lock popped, he folded the knife and dropped it into his jeans pocket. Entering in, he quickly locked the door again and looked around. He groaned to discover he was in a closet shaped like a triangle and filled with shelves containing stacks of folded linen. He heard the doors open and knew it was only a matter of time before they reached his closet. He would be found if he didn't hide and soon. Looking up, he felt a surge of hope. The closet had a suspended drop ceiling. If luck were with him, there would be a crawl space or at least, pipes or struts for him to hide in. It took him less than 10 seconds to climb one of the shelving units, push a tile aside and thrust his head into the space. "Bingo," he whispered to himself and pulled up on the wall that stuck a few inches above the ceiling. Replacing the tile, he looked around, turning his cell into a flashlight. Like most steel construction buildings, the walls ended approximately four inches above the grid used to hang the ceiling tiles. If he stayed on top of them, he could navigate most of the building without being seen. That is, as long as he didn't fall off. He had barely got the tile back in place when he heard the door jiggle followed by it being kicked open below.

Whew, that had been a close one. The guards walked around under him, checking the sharp corners then left, leaving the door open.

"Attention." Someone was announcing the hall. The voice was clear, coming through the crawl space from the main floor. "Everyone must move to the center of the room and empty your pockets onto the floor. I want it all - jewelry, money, watches, cell phones, everything. If you do not obey, you will die. If you try to run, you will die."

There were several moments of silence then the staccato of gunfire followed by screaming.

"You have been warned! Move, now!"

Toad swore. He could almost see the terrified people frozen uncertainty in the room. "Do what they say," he muttered to himself. "For God's sake, don't piss them off."

"It is a great honor to be chosen for God's mighty purpose. Today, we strike a blow at the heart of America's corrupt culture. Today, you will be a witness in this jihad against the infidels that destroy the minds of our children! This filth passed off as literature is nothing but the foulest of garbage. Today, it ends. Today, we destroy this affront in Allah's holy name."

A yell rose in the air followed by random gunfire

and screams. Toad adjusted his position slightly as he listened. Damn! He had hoped this was just a robbery, but it was much worse. There was no doubt about it; they were al-Bashir's radical extremists. He had heard the same rhetoric in every video the madman had spewed over the past few years.

Pulling out his cell, he checked it and saw it had no service. Most likely, the steel structure of the building interfered with reception. Swearing to himself, he shoved it back into his pocket. He had to get out of here and let the outside know what was going on. Determined to find a way to get help, he scooted along the wall, swinging around the steel support struts until it came to a junction. It ended after several feet at a wall that went all the way up. Unless he missed his guess, this would be the wall at the edge of the exhibition area. Bracing against it, he pulled out his knife and carefully pried a hole into the sheetrock wall in the corner. Just as he suspected, it was the main room. Glancing around, he saw people gathering in the center while several of the terrorists began to throw tables against the wall. They cleared a large path while another of their group scooped up cells, purses, and assorted items from the ground, shoveling them into bags. He spotted his friends and their women sitting on one edge. He swore softly. It was obvious River was afraid to run with his pregnant wife when he had no idea who or what was waiting on the main floor. He also knew Hick wouldn't have left them behind. It was too late now anyway. All except one of the exits were chained with guards standing in front of them. As he watched, a series of large crates were wheeled into the room through the unlocked door and moved to the corner where the two legs of the T shaped room met, about fifty feet from the knot of innocents. This was bad. This was so damn bad.

He scooted along the top of the wall toward the back, away from the main floor until he reached an outer wall. Leaning back, balanced on the little ledge, he pulled out his cell again and saw he finally had service - two bars only but it would be enough. Not knowing if there were any terrorists near him, he decided not to make any sound and began to type instead.

sadder ctr Phoenix. fedora cell. 10-12 terrorists. 100-150 hostages. i'm underground. Riv / Hick inside. exits sealed except one. possible explosives. advise.

He pressed send then silenced his phone.

Within five minutes, the device vibrated, and the screen lit up. It was a message from Bruiser.

Stay put. Bringing Bravo. ETA 90.

CHAPTER 16

Everything was going precisely to plan.

The man could barely contain his glee as the truck slammed into the front of the Center with a boom that shook the surrounding buildings. He watched as various emergency workers appeared on the scene. Each time one tried to enter the building; they were forced back with yells and gunfire. It took several additional deaths before they listened and concentrated on the carnage outside the building.

Zero Hour

Phoenix emergency services were working diligently to remove the hundreds of injured people that had been waiting for the doors to open as quickly as possible. A large panel truck had backed over the waiting crowd and rammed itself in the doorway. Moments later, the facade collapsed as the truck exploded burying the front in a pile of rock and glass. The police were trying to restore some order and clear out the area to minimize more causalities. Three emergency workers lay on the ground covered in sheets from their attempt to breach the building. Though they could not see the shooter, it was obvious they were being watched very closely.

Bravo team had been on site for twenty minutes now and was diligently collecting any data they could. They knew very little of what was going on inside. What they did know came courtesy of Toad holed up somewhere inside. Bruiser and Wolf stared at the blueprints spread out before them in the room they had commandeered in the Regency Inn behind the Sadder Performance and Exhibition Center. "This is the main exposition floor," Wolf stabbed at the large area. "They have shut down the entire floor, chained the exits and have the hostages here, in the center. The front was glass and stone. It's collapsed making an entry via the doors impossible."

"Are we sure this is Fedora? He always blows shit up and then rants afterward," Mozart growled as he glared at the plans.

"Toad thinks so. He said it was the same babble.

I'm not positive what's holding them back, but you can bet your ass there's a reason." Bruiser assured them.

Abe, Cookie, Finch, and Railroad marched through the door. The four of them were covered in grime with sweaty streaks trickling down their faces. The temperature was steadily climbing in the Phoenix sun making every step exhausting. Thankfully the air was still on in the center, or the increased heat could make the situation worse. The last thing they needed was short tempers on top of the already volatile state.

"Sit-Rep," Wolf barked. He and Bruiser shared leadership for the group working in tandem like a well-oiled machine.

"Good news and bad. Good news is the civilians who were upstairs when they hit are all evacuated through the upper balcony and down to the patio. That's a few hundred less potential casualties. Damn good that they chose today instead of tomorrow. Saturday is the biggest day, and there would have been thousands here. The bad news is, the doors at the stairwells are all sealed and the dogs hit on C4 on each one. The elevators are stopped, and the power's cut. They locked the doors going into the hall," Abe reported as he pointed to the plans spread out on the table. "They have wireless cameras installed at each door. It's going to be tough getting inside. They saw us snooping around and threatened to kill the hostages if we didn't get back. Toad confirmed via text there are cameras inside as well."

"That's not all Toad found out." Bruiser dropped his cell on the plans.

Benny leaned over and read the text out loud. "I overheard the guards talking. They are waiting for a bigger media presence. The leader, who calls himself Amir, plans on blowing the place on national television for maximum impact. He wants the world to see the U.S. fail on a grand scale."

"Mother humper," Finch muttered. "It's a suicide mission. They have no intention of letting the hostages go. That also explains why they didn't just blow it allowing most of the potential victims escape. They are opting for exposure to a larger body count."

"We need to buy some time. If they are waiting for a bigger media push, then we close down that avenue. Cowboy, you handle it."

"On it, Bruise."

Damn, but it was good to have Cowboy back

with them, if only for a short time. He had been getting ready to leave for the airport when Toad's message came. Immediately, he canceled his flight and was ready to go with them. Toad, Hick, and River were brothers and SEALs never left SEALs behind. Ever.

"We've got a slight advantage," Wolf reminded them. "We've got three on the inside."

"Yeah but we're only in contact with one of them," Railroad reminded them. "And I have an idea on how we can fix that."

Before Railroad could tell them, the door flew open and several men entered, approaching the table. The team bristled as one of them eyed them warily. "Christopher Feltzer, Homeland Security."

A tall man wearing a dark blue suit stepped out from behind him. "Dave Ballard, FBI. My team is on the way. Thank you, but we have it from here."

"Oh, hell no."

"This is bullshit."

"Forget it."

Bruiser threw up his hand to quiet the outcry from his fellow SEALs. "With all due respect, Feltzer, we're not going anywhere. You can work with us, or we can work alone, but we're staying. Two of our team members are in there along with an ex-member and their women. We're not standing back and watching from the sidelines." He shook his head emphatically. "Besides, the U.S. military has been chasing Haafiz al-Bashir for years. We are pretty sure this is a sleeper cell organized by him. If we have any chance of finding where that bastard is hiding, we're going to need new intel. One of them in there has to know where he is."

"This is our show, Marine. We'll let you know if we need you." Ballard snarled.

The team stiffened. "We'll see about that. And, we're SEALs, not Marines." Wolf stalked off pulling his cell out. He made a call, talked into the mouth-piece then hung up. Turning back, he crossed his arms. Ten minutes of standoff ended as the cell in Feltzer's pocket went off. Pointing to the Fed, he deadpanned, "Your boss wants to talk to you."

Feltzer's eyes widened in confusion. Taking out the cell, he pressed it to his ear. Feltzer's confusion turned to outright shock. "Yes, Sir." He listened a few more moments then nodded. "I understand, Sir." He punched the phone and dropped it into his pocket. "I don't know how you did it, but we're working with you." He turned to look at his counterpart. "They are taking point. The order came from all the way up." Narrowing his eyes his voice lowered. "But, you don't make a move without keeping me in the loop. Got it?"

"Got it," they answered then turned back to the papers stacked on the table.

"Go ahead, Railroad. What's your idea?"

Toad knew they were in deep shit. From the little bit he had been able to piece together from the guards' chatter, the clock was ticking down, and he didn't want anyone near here when the timer hit zero. It was going to be up to him to get this situation under control as soon as possible. He was their wild card, their ace in the hole. The terrorists didn't know he was there. The plan Railroad and the others had hatched was a good one, but it was going to be tricky to instigate. So far, all was going to plan as he quietly pulled out the equipment he would need from the media center that faced the smaller stage sitting behind the bathrooms on one side of the exhibition floor. Toad was an expert when it came to surveillance equipment, and they were going to need all the tricks he could pull out of his hat to make this work. Glancing over his shoulder every few minutes, listening for any guards approaching, he worked the in-house equipment until he found the signal they used to monitor the cameras placed on the floor. "Twelve. It'd take too long to close them all down and loop back," he muttered to himself. Instead, he concentrated on the ones on one side only, creating a ten-minute loop for the two trained on the elevator and the corridor outside. He winced when the guard wandered through the scene, paused at the elevator and peered into space. Turning around, he sauntered out of the view, crossing through the second feed and disappeared. Toad didn't have time to edit it out. Instead, he completed the task and broadcasted the signal back to the feeds. Holding his breath, he listened then let it out when it appeared nobody noticed the loops being activated. Perfect.

Slipping out of the room, he peered down the hall, checking the way to ensure that nobody was there. The guard stood in the doorway of the elevator, his gun pointing up, head tipped to the side as he studied the space. Shit. What he wouldn't do for a weapon right now. Drawing out the knife, he pulled open the tiny blade and gripped it tightly in his hand. It was all he had, and he hated to defile Rayna's gift like this, but he didn't have much choice. One of the two of them wasn't walking away and he'd be damned if it was him. Taking a breath, Toad inched down the hall then struck. He grabbed the terrorist around the head, slapping his hand over his mouth as the fist clutching the knife slammed down, jarring the assault rifle from his grasp. It clattered to the floor of the hall. He winced at the noise, but he couldn't help it now. Hopefully, there were no other guards nearby to hear it. Quickly, he plunged the short blade of the pocket knife directly into the side of the man's neck, severing the jugular. Pushing him forward into the elevator, he kept the man pinned against the wall until he quit struggling and slumped to the floor in a growing pool of blood. Drawing the knife out, he wiped it on the man's sleeve, closed it and returned it to his pocket. Letting out a soft warble of a whistle, he glanced up at the ceiling hatch opened and a pair of legs thrust through. Quickly, Dude dropped to the floor and reached up. A black bag was lowered, and he grabbed it, stepping to the side. Railroad dropped through followed by Wolf. Railroad unzipped the bag, pulling out a Sig Sauer and handed it over. Toad checked it, popped magazine into the butt and shoved the pistol into the waistband of his jeans. He then took the earwig and mic set and put them on. Railroad held out a plastic bag containing two more Sigs, four magazines, and two mics.

"Ready?"

"Yeah let's get this party started," Toad muttered.

CHAPTER 17

The man kept silent vigilance from the balcony. He had warned Amir of the search party an hour ago and watched them leave quickly shortly afterward. Now the roof was clear and none dared to approach. He smiled. There will be only one outcome from this day.

- 2 hours

Every eye in the room was locked on the man walking back and forth, muttering to himself. He made a slow, tight circle, stopping every few moments to stare at a group of monitors that was sitting on one of the artist's tables. As he made his circuit, his booted feet crunched over swag, books and other litter strewn over the floor. Even from where Hick and the others sat in a group, he could hear him talking to himself.

"Where are the trucks? Where are the reporters?" He stopped, looked at the screen then resumed pacing. "There must be more. Time is almost up."

"What do you think is going on," Hick muttered to River.

River's eyes watched the man as he curled his arms around Joselyn settled between his legs on the floor. Everyone in the room had been herded into the middle and all the furniture thrown carelessly against the walls. Every so often, a chair would shift, tumbling down the pile and making one of the hostages cry out in fear. Without taking his eyes off the leader, River answered. "I'm thinking they are keeping this quiet, not giving him the audience he craves. You heard him spilling his bilge earlier. He is looking for a big audience to watch this crapfest."

"God, I've got to pee," Annabeth muttered. "My bladder is ready to float off. You may want to back up, Hick. I'd hate to wash you down when it lets go."

She sat much like Joselyn did, back to his front with his legs cradled on either side. He wrapped his arms around her and squeezed gently. "I'll see what I can do," he muttered into her ear. Scooting back, he slowly rose to his feet, his hands high in the air. "Excuse me."

One of the six men roving around the area hurried over, pointing his assault rifle at Hick. "Sit!" He screamed at him.

"We've been here for a couple of hours, and some of the ladies need a bathroom break. It's going to get smelly in here really fast if you don't let them go to the restroom."

He heard Annabeth mutter to Joselyn, "He's channeling *Die Hard*."

In answer, the man raised the gun and brought the butt down on Hick's shoulder. He hissed and doubled over as red sprouted in the area. "Sit down!"

"What's going on?" The leader hurried over as Hick dropped to his knees with his hands up.

"He says the women need to go to the bathroom."

The leader glared at Hick who knelt, boldly staring at the man with barely concealed hostility burning in his gaze. "It's about to get messy in here really fast," he said in an even tone. "Could you please let them take a break? I don't want to spend my last few hours smelling urine."

The leader touched the bloom of crimson darkening Hick's shirt. "What is this? Why are you bleeding?" He turned to the guard that had struck him. "What did you do? I told you to keep them quiet."

Hmmm. No trace of an accent. The leader must be home grown. "It's nothing. I hurt myself a few days ago. I popped a stitch," Hick ground out.

The man pushed the neck of Hick's shirt aside, exposing a white bandage with blood in the middle. Letting it go, he stepped back.

"So about the bathroom?" Hick asked.

"Very well." The leader pointed to two of the guards. "Take them to the bathroom eight at a time."

Annabeth, Joselyn, and another six women walked ahead of the two terrorists out the only unlocked door and disappeared around the corner. Hick waited impatiently until they re-emerged several moments later. Likewise, another group was chosen and then a third.

When the fourth group returned, one of the women broke off and approached them. Dropping to the floor beside Annabeth, she watched the next group disappear. When they did, she turned to him and whispered. "I have something for you."

She looked up again and made sure no-one was paying attention to her before she continued in a low tone. "When I got to the bathroom, there was a man in there. I about had a heart attack when I opened the door, and he was squatting on the toilet. Thank God the guards stayed outside the door. He said his name was Toad and told me help is on the way. Then he showed me a picture of you on his phone and asked me to give you this." She pressed two small items into his hand. Hick looked down and saw they were mini earwigs like the ones they used on missions. That could only mean the team was here. Toad was able to alert them. There were no microphones, but at least he could hear what was going on.

"Thank you," he whispered back. "You're very brave to do this."

"Getting out of this alive that would be thanks enough." She grinned slyly. "Unless Toad's single?"

Hick chuckled which pulled the attention of the guard returning with another group of women. Carefully making his face a mask of indifference, he focused on the floor. After a moment, another group of women was taken.

"Yeah, he's single. After this is over, you should talk to him."

"Thanks, I'll do that."

The woman scooted off. Hick looked over at River and saw a quizzical look on his face. Glancing around to ensure no-one was looking, he tossed the second earwig over then stuffed his own into his ear. Relief flooded through him when he heard Wolf's voice.

"We've got eyes on you. Fist for no, flat for yes. Can you hear me clear?"

Both of the men flattened their palms to the floor.

"Good. Here's the plan."

Ten minutes later, the last of the women returned from their bathroom breaks. Starting from the other side, the terrorists rounded up a group of men and escorted them to the bathroom. There were far fewer men than women so he knew it wouldn't take as long. When it came to their turn, River and Hick stood and allowed themselves to be pushed unceremoniously through the door and into the utility hall. Once inside, Hick made his way to the enclosed stall, bypassing the row of urinals.

"Where are you going?" One of the terrorists asked in a harsh tone. He motioned toward the others standing at the urinals.

"Man, I had tacos for lunch, my stomach is churning. If you want me to lay tracks in the urinal, okay, but it would be easier and a lot cleaner in the toilet."

After a momentary hesitation, he nodded. "Be quick," he snapped then leaned against the row of sinks. Hick went to the last stall and entered, shutting the door behind. Bracing on the toilet he quietly lifted the lid to the tank, grateful they hadn't upgraded the bathrooms to the tankless commodes many places now favored. Just as Wolf promised, there was a plastic bag.

He made a rude noise with his tongue. "Ahh.. yeah, that's much better. Sorry guys, more room out than in."

Ignoring the chorus of groans and complaints, Hick opened the bag, took out the two Sigs, magazines and microphones. Stuffing the mics and extra magazines into his pocket, he tossed the bag back into the tank and recovered it. Sitting on the toilet lid, he made another farting noise, dragging it out as he slid the magazine into the base of each Sig and engaged the safety. Stuffing one of the weapons into the waistband on the side of his jeans, he put the second in his pocket and pulled his shirttail out of his jeans down over them. The two extra magazines went into his other pocket. He stood, flushed the toilet and opened the door. Hunching over slightly, he wrapped his arms around his stomach as if it were hurting and stumbled out of the stall. The terrorist's eyes swept over him until he stood at the sink, washing his hands then drying them. River stood beside him, washing his hands as well. They watched their guard via the mirror until he turned away. Quickly, Hick slid the pocketed Sig out and over to River who took it and pushed it into his pocket. Shuffling along with the others, the two followed the rest of the hostages back out to the floor. Hick felt better. His team was here, watching their six and they had each a weapon.

Now, if they can just keep the leader from blowing them all to hell and back.

CHAPTER 18

The man took another drink from his water bottle as he watched the scene vigilantly. Since the initial breach, no more attempts had been made to enter the building. The walkie-talkie beside him remained silent. Time was about up. Even if the desired media presence didn't show, the bomb will cement today's actions in the minds of the entire world. The final stage was fast approaching.

- 4 hours

The roving guard slumped forward as Wolf pulled his KA-BAR out of the body and eased it to the ground. Without a word, Railroad grabbed him under the arms and dragged him into the tiny storage area to rest with the other three they had dispatched. Closing the door, he gave a nod to Wolf then joined Dude in a final sweep of the exterior area. Wolf joined Toad in the media center.

"How's it going?"

"Good. This is the last one." Toad lifted his chin toward the monitor he had rigged on the soundboard. He fiddled with the device until a picture zoomed into focus. "There," he declared triumphantly. "That's it. The exterior cameras are all looped back. We have the run of the outside."

"Great. Also, good job in finding that electrical service egress and disarming the alarms. It was a tight fit but at least we weren't seen."

Toad's lip lifted slightly. "Just another glorious day in the service."

Wolf chuckled and pressed the button on the mic. "We're ready." Leaving Toad to monitor the electronics, he joined the others at the elevator. Within moments, the hatch opened, and the rest of Bravo, minus Bruiser dropped in one by one. With his injured leg, Bruiser was staying back at the command center and coordinating things for them. Well, that and pacifying the Feds who were not happy at staying on the outside of this op. However, they finally conceded that the SEALs were better trained to handle the situation inside. That left the Feds with the task of finding who the watcher was that had alerted Amir of their presence earlier.

Carefully, the team worked their way to the small storage room. Dude and Cowboy disarmed the C4 packs that were on the chained access points. The defunct bombs sat on a shelf out of harm's way.

"How's it looking, Toad?"

"Clear," came the terse reply.

"It's a go." Wolf climbed up on the steel shelves and disappeared through the missing ceiling tile. Reaching the top of the wall, he moved along it quickly. Without looking behind him, he knew Abe, Cookie, Railroad, and Mozart followed. The rest of the team would stay on this side of the building. The only way to move from one side of the exhibition hall to the other without using the floor itself was via a small catwalk along the back wall of the room. Toad had found it earlier.

Once they traversed the spans, they went completely silent, using hand signals to coordinate their movements. It wasn't the first time he was grateful for the new ASL protocol that the SEALs had established. Being able to talk to the others without making a sound was a Godsend. Since this side contained the only door not chained and therefore would allow one of the remaining eight tangos to appear at any moment, it was beneficial to be able to relay orders silently.

Quickly, he signed to the others, and they dispersed to their assigned spots. Looking over at Cookie where he stood in the doorway, he gave the nod. It was almost time.

Hick listened to Bruiser as he ticked off the Sit-Rep through the coms in his ear. He and River had both been given the plan and knew all hell would break loose soon. He barely resisted the urge to look up at the walls and search for the holes he knew Railroad and Benny had made in them. They were the snipers today, watching over the situation with a trained eye. Railroad was a dead shot when it came to taking down targets with forty confirmed kills. He didn't know what Benny's record was, but if Wolf and Bruiser had decided he was the best man for the other nest, then nobody would second guess them. Even though they were a hybrid task force team, they all trusted each other explicitly.

The other deadliest sniper in the building, River,

sat a few feet away. He had Joselyn in his arms, holding her tightly as he watched the movements of their captors. He had retired from the SEALs last year, but Hick had no qualms that the man retained his skill set. Even now, he could see the quiet steel as he assessed and calculated in his mind all the scenarios of 'what if.'

Hick's attention returned to Annabeth pressed tightly against his front. She was trembling again. Wrapping his arms around her, he whispered in her ear, "Shhh, Georgia. It's all going to be okay. Just remember, when the shooting starts, flatten yourself on the ground. River and I are trained, we can handle anything. Your job is to keep low and take care of yourself."

The mass of messy red curls in front of his face nodded slightly. He could feel the lump of the Sig Saur pressed between them, and it comforted him. Granted, he would feel a lot better if Annabeth and Joselyn weren't even there at all, but he'd take what he could. His and River's job was to keep an eye on things inside and to be back up as a last resort. If things went ass up, and they very well could, it was their duty to ensure the safety of the hostages.

He knew the doors were no longer rigged due to the chatter going through the coms, but the big crate sitting on the floor near the leader was troubling. It was the wildcard here. If it weren't for it, the team would already have swarmed the room. They didn't know if the crate was rigged with a dead man's switch. River thought it probably was since all of these men were prepared to die for their cause anyway. The question was, how many innocents would be going with them? Hick hardened his resolve. None, if the SEALs could help it.

"I still don't see anything, but he keeps his hand under the table," Railroad murmured.

"With the contents hidden in the box, I can't tell what kind of device it is," Dude returned. "It could be C4 like the others. It could be a dirty bomb. Hell, it could be a firecracker for all we know." Hick could hear the frustration in his voice.

"Are we sure that it's not on a remote with someone else handling the trigger?" Cowboy whispered.

"I have all the feeds captured. If someone is watching off-site, they see business as usual. We're locked down."

Hick looked over at River. The older man shook his head slightly. Hick raised one eyebrow causing River to glare. With a shrug, he gave him a smirk then turned his attention back to the leader. Curling one hand behind his back, he raised his middle finger in a salute.

"Hold on. Hick's trying to say something."

Slowly he signed his idea in crude, rudimentary motions. He knew Railroad would be watching from his position on the wall.

"Be... ready... getting... attention..." Railroad translated.

"Oh hell," Cowboy swore into the com. "Don't do something stupid, Hick. We can still do this even with not knowing what's in the crate."

Hick leaned in and whispered in Annabeth's ear. "Hey beautiful, we are about to have our first fight. Just go with it. We need to pull the leader's attention. If I say, 'that's enough' then we stop."

The four-letter word that erupted from Annabeth's mouth shocked him. He had never heard her use that one before. Hugging her tightly, he whispered, "It'll be okay. Trust me. Just be loud, obnoxious and stay low."

"This is a bad idea, Hick. I swear to God; you get killed, I'm getting an Ouija board, pulling your ghost back into your body and killing you myself." River growled. Whispering into Joselyn's ear, the two scooted back away from Hick and Annabeth. He then maneuvered Joselyn behind him as much as was possible. "When the shit hits the fan, you flatten to the ground, Jos. Alright?"

"Okay," she replied in a shaky voice.

"Ready?" Hick murmured into Annabeth's hair.

She shook her head, hesitated then slowly nodded. "I love you, Hick. Just remember, I die because of this cockamamie idea of yours, I'm so haunting your sexy ass for the rest of your life."

He snorted then leaned back, tucking the gun back into his waistband and covering it with his shirttails. Taking a deep breath, he started.

"You know, we could be sitting by a fireplace, sipping drinks and listening to some nice music instead of this bullshit if you would have just listened to me."

"Well, this is my job, Levi. I thought you understood it. I can't just throw everything into the wind."

"That's a given, you never do anything spontaneous, Annabeth. Just for once, I'd love for you to not have a thousand lists with every moment of every day planned to a T."

They had started out in a regular tone, but it had slowly increased. Backing away from Hick, Annabeth slid around until she could see his face.

"At least I have a plan. You never do. It's always fly by the seat of your pants."

"I don't need plans for every second of every day. I get enough of that shit with my job. When we are together, I need to have a little room, a little spontaneity."

Their argument had drawn the attention of every person in the room. Two of the guards had hurried over to them. "Be quiet," one hissed at them and drew his rifle up.

"See what you've done Hick, now you are going to get us all killed. How is that for spontaneity? Is that random enough for you?" Her voice had become a high toned screech.

"Typical, Annabeth, taking everything I say and turning it around. I am not the bad guy here. All I wanted was a nice quiet evening with you. Is that too much to ask?"

"If you are asking to have your nice quiet evening on the weekend of the busiest time of my year, it is. I already give you every moment you request. Why can't that ever be enough?"

Hick barely kept the grin off his face. He watched the leader stand at the table next to the crate then walk around it. He picked up a pistol and hurried over. The other guards had moved closer but had their eyes trained on the scene playing out between Hick and Annabeth.

"It could be enough if you would just let me see I am enough."

She threw her hands up. "Oh, so we are going to do this now? Seriously, Levi? You want to air out all our dirty laundry right at this moment?"

A man stood up and marched over to them. Sticking a finger into Hick's chest, he screamed, "Shut up! Are you trying to get us killed?"

"Andrew!" Annabeth said in a strained voice.

He narrowed his eyes at her. "And you. My God, Annabeth. Do you think this is the place to discuss your lover's quarrel? These men are going to kill us. Do you understand just how incredibly stupid your actions are at this moment? You need to sit your redneck ass down tell Mr. Green Jeans there to shove a handful of cornbread in his mouth and shut up!"

The room gasped in shock at the bilge flying from the author's lips. Hick stood and glared at him. "You can say whatever you want about me, but if I ever hear you saying another word to Annabeth, I will show you what Mr. Green Jeans can do with a handful of cornbread."

"Hick," River muttered. He had stood as well, pulling Joselyn firmly behind him. The leader arrived, holding his pistol firmly, watching the scene with a frown firmly on his face.

"All of you sit down." The guard took a step between the two. He raised the gun and pressed it into Andrew's chest. "Sit, or I will kill you. I will kill you both."

Fury apparently had fried the man's brain. He roared at the man. "If you are going to kill someone, kill them. They are nobody, nothing. She's a second rate agent and him...he's just some nobody who keeps her smiling. I'm an artist, a one of a kind star. I'll be remembered as a god among authors." He wrapped his fingers around the muzzle and shoved. "Now get that thing away from me!"

The sound of gunfire filled the room. Shock registered on Andrew's face as a huge hole exploded through his chest spraying blood to those standing nearby. In an instant, people screamed, and the room exploded in gunshots.

In short, hell had descended.

CHAPTER 19

With the first shots fired from the building across the way, the man knew things had taken a turn for the worse. Training his binoculars down into the street, he saw a group of men wearing jackets proclaiming they were FBI enter the hotel. He frowned and began stuffing his things into a bag. It was time to return home and report directly to The Left Hand.

Getting caught in America was not an option.

-4.5 hours

Andrew was dead.

Annabeth blinked in shock, watching his body crumple in slow motion.

He fell to the floor, his hand flopping out, palm

up on top of her foot. She looked down into the vacant depth of his eyes and still the same three words echoed in her head.

Andrew was dead.

She took a hurried leap back away from the corpse and screamed in horror. The man was a pain in the ass and the bane of her professional existence, but she never wanted him actually to die. In her hurry to get away, she stumbled back onto a small pile of debris and slipped. Her butt made contact with the unforgiving floor, jarring her teeth until they rattled in her head. She barely acknowledged the jolt. Adrenaline dumped into her system making her heart race. Her eyes stayed trained on the body of her client staring up at the ceiling only a few feet from her.

"Annabeth!"

She dimly registered her name as an arm curled around her chest and pulled her to her feet. "Get up," a voice punctured the haze of her stupor.

"Okay, Hick," she murmured but couldn't get her body to obey. The arm pulled at her insistently until finally, she climbed to her feet.

His body molded itself to her, wrapping one arm around her waist tightly. His breath fanned the strands of hair that had escaped the severe bun she had put in it this morning. "Move," he hissed.

She wrinkled her brow in confusion. Why was Hick so abrupt? She turned her head to ask then spied someone standing a few feet from her, pistol drawn and focused on them. He stared at her intently with barely restrained fury in his eyes. Eyes she recognized even through the fuzzy haze of shock that pounded in her mind. Wait. If that was Hick then who had her snuggled up against him?

"Let her go," Hick growled at them. "Let her go, and you'll live through this."

In response, she felt something hard press into her ribs. She hissed in fear and tried to twist away. She couldn't move. Glancing over her shoulder, she saw it was the leader of the terrorists. Well, shit. This can't be good.

"Move back, Mr. Green Jeans," the man snarled. "Or she dies."

Hick shook his head. "Let her go, asshole. I'm warning you."

He laughed tightly, the sound loud in her ears.

"Hick?" she whispered uncertainly.

"It's ok, honey." His eyes never left the face of her captor. His hands never wavered as he stared down the barrel of the gun at them.

The terrorist pulled her back with him. She stumbled, her feet slipping on the slick papers littering the floor. He stopped then began to move to the left, toward the front. Something warm dripped down her shoulder and splattered on her hand. She looked down and saw blood covering her front. Andrew's blood. There was so much of it. Another drop fell, and she watched it mingle with the others. She wanted the coppery mess off her and barely resisted the urge to scrub her hands on her skirt.

"My dry cleaner is going to quit," she said under her breath.

"Shut up, woman," the man barked in her ear.

"You're going nowhere. Let the woman go. We have the room locked down." Hick prowled forward keeping steps with them.

The terrorist's breathing was faster than ever, panting against the side of her face. She shuddered. She wouldn't have minded Hick growling into her ear, but this guy? Not so much. She must have said so out loud because Hick's lips twitched slightly. "I'll pant on you later," he soothed her.

"There will be no later. She is going to die. Stop now, or I will kill her right before your eyes."

"And you die too, asshole. Look around. You're leaving here in a body bag if you don't let her go."

"I'm prepared. I came here today knowing I would give my life for my beliefs. Are you willing to watch this woman die?" Spittle flew from the man's lips.

The words finally registered in Annabeth's addled mind. With the realization, fear slammed into her with the force of a semi tractor. She gasped, and her head felt light. Looking around, she saw two others dressed in the uniforms that Hick had called BDUs or battle dress uniforms. Each had a serious looking rifle pointed at them. They slowly advanced toward Hick, matching him step for step but moving in an oblique direction spreading out behind him. Past them, Cowboy and River were herding the others out the door. She heard them urging the hostages to move faster. Another SEAL hurried over the messy floor to the crate. He dropped his rifle then stared at the wooden container. Even from this distance, she could see several fingers of his left hand were mangled.

"Duuude?"

One of the men approaching Hick hissed the word but didn't take his eyes off her.

"It's going to take a few minutes, Wolf." Dude returned from beside the crate. He took one more glance at the object and advanced toward the table containing the monitors.

"Get away from there," her captor screeched. He pulled the gun up and pressed it painfully against Annabeth's temple. "He gets closer to Allah's Fire; she will die."

"Dude! Back away," Hick ground out.

Annabeth saw him stop only a few inches from the table then take several steps back. Silence fell on the room as the last of the hostages were ushered out leaving her, the terrorist, Hick and the three SEALs she hadn't met.

"Your hostages are gone. Let her go," Wolf's voice was growly and low. "You aren't getting out of here with her."

"I never intended to," came the gleeful reply. "I knew today would be the one where I finally meet Allah."

"You failed," Hick snapped out. "The hostages are gone. How is Allah and Haafiz al-Bashir going to feel when you die for nothing?"

"Soon, this building will still fall. When it does, my name will be called out. I will be remembered as one of Allah's great soldiers. *Allahu akbar!*"

"There's a timer!" Dude yelled then swore. "This

needs to end now. I don't know how much time we have left to disarm."

"Not enough," the man sneered.

Annabeth listened to the exchange. The more this jerk spoke, the more pissed she got. Hick and the others were heroes. They risked their lives every day to bring down fascists like this one pressed against her back. She would be damned if she allowed this jackass to hurt them or anyone else.

"Take the shot," she said in an even tone.

Hick's brow wrinkled, and he shook his head slightly. "No."

"Take the freaking shot, Hick. Don't let this asshole win."

"Shut up!" The terrorist screamed in her ear then shoved the barrel of the gun harder against her temple, making her head cant to the side.

"Go on Levi Salter. Take the damned shot. Don't let him hurt anyone else. Don't let his hatred win. Take. The. Shot."

"Georgia," Hick's voice was haunted.

"I love you too," she said with a smile then closed her eyes.

She heard the shots.

She felt the pain.

She succumbed to the nothing.

"Annabeth!"

Hick's heart stopped in his chest as he watched the love of his life collapse to the floor. Panic sliced through him as he lunged forward, kicking the pistol away from the leader and dropped beside her. "No, no, no," he chanted as he reached her still body. Gently, he cupped the back of her neck and turned her face toward him. Dark lashes lay on ashen cheeks, her coral lips standing out in stark contrast. Tenderly, he swept a lock of her crimson hair back from her face. It was stiff with Andrew's blood already drying. She was too still and her face much too pale. Her lips had taken a blue tone, and he couldn't see her chest rise. Gathering her limp form into his arms, he held her close. God, how would he survive? How will he live without her?

Mozart dropped to his knees beside them. "Let me see," he said quietly.

Hick ignored him. Instead, he rocked quietly, whispering to her, telling her how much he loved her.

"Dammit, Hick, let me see her," Mozart pulled at his arm.

"How will I live without her, Mozart?"

"He's in shock," Abe said as he dropped beside him. "Mozart needs to see her. Let her go, Hick."

Hands grabbed at his arms, trying to snatch his Georgia from him. He fought against them, snarling as they tried to pry her from his grasp.

"She's not dead, Hick. She's still breathing." Toad murmured as he laid a hand on his friend's shoulder. "Let Mozart have her. Let him save her life."

Wolf stood over them with his rifle pointed to the ground. "We need to get her stabilized enough to get her out of here. Dude and Cowboy are working on the bomb, but we don't know how much time we have."

Recognition finally dawned on him. Hick gritted his teeth and allowed them to pull her from his embrace. His eyes never left as Toad laid her flat on her back and Mozart assessed her. Rolling her over, Mozart found the entry point. Grabbing a stack of gauze squares from the medi-bag at his side, he pressed it tightly against it and the exit wound on the front of her shoulder. The team waited with baited breath as he worked. "It's clear through. I've slowed the bleeding for the moment, but we need to get her to the hospital ASAP. She's in a bad way."

"Got it!" Dude called out from the front of the room, "and with two minutes to spare. Not even movie of the week worthy."

Hick didn't care about the bomb or that Dude had it diffused. He didn't care that they were less than two minutes from becoming ashes. He didn't even care that the front of his shirt was soaked with blood. None of that mattered to him. Everything that was precious to him lay on the floor next to a dead terrorist, pouring her life out into Mozart's blood-stained hands. He was dimly aware of others, his team, police, and federal agents swarming the room, but he kept his eyes focused entirely on her.

"Dammit!"

For the second time tonight, his heart stuttered.

Mozart yelled, "I don't feel her pulse."

Toad dropped to his knees beside her, pressed two fingers to the uninjured side of her neck and frowned. Quickly, he cupped his hands, one on top of the other and began chest compressions. "Come on, Bethy. Breathe."

Hick felt Cowboy and River grab him and pull him back away from the trio. They were trying to make him leave her. He couldn't. Not now, not ever.

Yanking his arms out of their grasp, he crawled over, picked up her limp hand and stroked it.

"Hick!"

"No! I'm not leaving her. You can court-martial me if you have to for disobeying orders, Bruise, but I am not moving away from her." He turned back to her and spoke. "Come on Georgia. Come back to me. You can't leave. Not now. Please. God, please don't take my Georgia," he begged out loud. He didn't care who heard him. If it made him weak, so what? If it meant getting her back, he would do whatever was necessary; his pride be damned. His eyes filled with water and he let the tears fall. He just didn't care.

He rocked slowly, holding her hand against his chest. "You can't leave me, honey. You can't. I have all these plans. I got the cabin for us up in the mountains. I was going to surprise you. It has everything - hot tub, fireplace, a gorgeous view overlooking the valley. The agent said there's a family of deer that will eat right out of your hand. It even has a concierge chef to cook for us so we wouldn't have to leave. I have it all planned." He lifted her hand to his lips and pressed a tender kiss to her knuckles. "All for you, my Georgia. It's all for you."

The room was quiet, filled only with the sounds of Toad grunting as he continued to do CPR. Then it was broken with Hick's baritone as he sang his version of their song.

I said, Georgia, oh Georgia. No peace will I find. You're my Georgia, sweet Georgia, forever on my mind.

Toad stopped compressions as Hick's song ended. Mozart pressed two bloody fingers against the carotid artery. Relief filled his face. "There's a pulse. Where the hell are those paramedics?"

In answer, two men appeared with a gurney and took over her care. Hick allowed them to pull her hand out of his grasp, but he never was further than a couple of feet away as they loaded her onto a backboard and started an IV. Once they had her secured, they placed her on the stretcher and rolled her out a side door. Within moments, she was lifted into the ambulance. Hick began to climb in but was stopped by one of the medics. "Are you related?"

"No, but if you think for one minute you are going to keep me out of there, you're insane. Where she goes, I go."

The man must have seen something dangerous in Hick's eyes for he nodded tightly. "Then ride in the front. I don't need you crowding me in back if there's an emergency."

Hick whirled around and hopped into the front. Glancing back through the tiny window, he saw the paramedics lock her stretcher into the bay. One jumped into the back; the other climbed into the front. The siren was loud as they roared out of the parking lot. Hick didn't look back at his team standing there watching them leave. His eyes were on the still form in the back, thanking God for every breath she took.

CHAPTER 20

It had taken days, but the man had finally worked his way to the border. He stayed hunched down, watching the line of trees that marked the change from one nation to another. As soon as his contact appeared, he would leave this hated country behind and take his place with Haafiz al-Bashir, the Left Hand of Allah once again. The money that had exchanged hands would ensure a smooth crossing.

Movement alerted him to another's presence. He smiled and gave the signal. It wouldn't be much longer. Stepping out, he lifted his hand to hail the handler who would escort him across.

- 2 days

Bing Bong... Bing Bong...

What was that irritating noise?

Annabeth tried to open her eyes, but they were glued shut. She frowned as the annoying dings continued to invade her mind. Couldn't someone turn that off? She raised her hand, or at least she thought she raised her hand to wipe her eyes and try to force them open, but the darn thing just jiggled a bit then lay still. She tried to lick her lips, but her mouth was dry. None of this made sense. Why couldn't she move and what was wrong with her eyes and mouth?

Anger surged up in her as that damned noise continued to her left then suddenly it ended. Mustering all her strength, she concentrated on her eyes and forced them to open a sliver finally then slammed them shut again. The room was blindingly bright with a light shining right above her, stabbing her as if the particles of light were tiny blades. She groaned and wished she had kept them firmly shut.

"Georgia?"

She knew that voice. Golden brown eyes, the color of warm caramel appeared in her mind followed by dirty blond hair and a pair of beautiful dimples. A thousand memories crowded into her mind of a sexy, well-built man cuddling her tightly against him. It felt right. It felt like home. It felt like...

"Hick?" she croaked.

"Oh thank God. Yeah, baby. I'm here." He took her hand in his and gripped it tightly. "Can you open your eyes?"

"Bright," she whispered and barely shook her head. "Too much."

She heard the sound of a switch. "Try it now."

Slowly she cracked her eyelids just a bit and sighed in relief when the horrid light was gone. The comfort of darkness engulfed her. "Water," she croaked. Her eyes followed him as he turned to the right and picked up a cup sitting on the rolling table. Holding the straw to her lips, he told her to take small sips. At this point, that was all she could do.

"Honey, you scared me to death. Please don't ever do that again."

"'k," she agreed then closed her heavy eyelids. "Tired."

He leaned down and pressed his lips to her cheek. "Sleep now. I'll see you when you wake."

The nothing claimed her.

The next time she woke, the room was dark except for a glow coming from the television mounted on the wall. A re-run of *Criminal Minds* played on the screen with the volume down low. A soft snort sounded from her right. She looked over to see Hick laying back in a recliner sound asleep. Annabeth studied his face, noticing dark circles under his eyes and worry lines etched on his forehead. The blue scrubs he wore were wrinkled as if he had had been wearing them for days. As she watched, his chin dropped, and a half snore/half gasp shot out. It was so funny she giggled then groaned when her chest hurt.

"Annabeth?"

She looked at the foot of her bed to where Grace was curled up in a chair. Her sister stood quickly and hurried to the bedside. Gently she swept Annabeth's hair out of her face and behind her ear. Worry engulfed her.

"Gracie," Annabeth whispered the childhood name. "What are you doing here? Where are Kenseth and Elliot?"

"They are at the hotel. God, Beth, we've been so worried about you. How are you feeling?"

"Drugged," she replied. "Where am I? How long have I been out?"

"Banner University Hospital in Phoenix and you've been unconscious for two days." Hick stood on the other side of the bed. He looked relieved, and the smile that brightened his face lit up the room.

"Hey there, Georgia." He leaned down and pressed a gentle kiss to her lips.

It was tender and sweet, and it made her belly clench appreciatively. Love flooded her as she looked up at him. "Is everyone okay? Toad, Railroad and the others?"

"One of the many reasons I love you. You're always worried about others. None of the team got hurt. Everyone is fine. They have to report in the morning, so they left for Cali this afternoon."

"And you?"

Hick shrugged. "I have some time off. They can handle things without me for a few days."

"Hick?"

His thumb made circles on her knuckles. It was both soothing and relaxing. She felt her muscles melt. "What happened?"

He frowned. "We can talk about it later. Right now you need to rest."

Annabeth's eyes narrowed. "I've been resting for two days. I want to know what happened. I remember the convention and some terrorists. You and I were arguing, and then it just goes blank."

He sighed heavily then pulled the recliner over until it was beside her bed. Taking her hand, he carefully maneuvered the IV line until it was out of the way.

On the other side, Grace tucked the covers up and smoothed them gently. "I've heard this story, so I think I'll go get some coffee and call Kenseth." She leaned down and kissed Annabeth's forehead. When the door had closed, Annabeth looked to Hick quizzically.

He drew in a breath and sat on the edge of the chair so that his face was even with hers. Guilt radiated off him in thick, cloying waves. Reaching over, he traced the side of her face with his finger. "The fight? That was a fake. We were trying to distract the leader of the terrorists to get him away from the bomb. You know that, right?"

"Yeah, that feels right."

He let out a breath of relief. "Good. God, I'm so sorry. I shouldn't have gotten you involved. How can you ever forgive me?"

"Already forgiven, love, I helped you because I wanted to. There's no guilt involved." She wrinkled her brow. "Did Andrew...?"

"Yeah. That part was true too. I'm sorry."

Annabeth felt tightness behind her eyes. "He was a jerk, but he didn't deserve that. None of us did."

She took a cleansing breath. "So, what else happened?"

"I can give you the short version. The leader was a homegrown terrorist named Roger Hartman. He dropped out of college and spent three years in the Middle East, learning from Haafiz al-Bashir. When he returned home, he set to work recruiting a sleeper cell. The convention was exactly the stage they needed to air their hatred and cultural purity agenda. Toad was able to sneak the rest of the team in. We started the argument which pulled all the guards from the edges and into the middle of the room where snipers could get a bead on them. The team took action and dropped the guards. Hartman saw what was happening and grabbed you before they could get him. He hid behind you, not giving the snipers a good shot. You were so brave, ready to die to keep the others safe. You stood there and told me to shoot you. Jesus, woman, there's no way I could have done that."

"If you didn't shoot me, then who did?"

"Hartman. Railroad caught him peeking out from behind you and shot him. Hartman pulled the trigger as he fell, shooting you through the back and out your shoulder. You were so lucky, baby. So damned lucky. The bullet nicked the pericardium which filled with blood and squeezed your heart. Ah, God, how could you ever forgive me for putting you into that situation?"

Annabeth could see the terror on his face at the thought of how close she had been to death. She shivered in reaction. It had been close, too close. She swallowed and placed a hand on his shoulder. "There's nothing to forgive."

"Yes, there is. I got you involved. You almost..."

"But I didn't, and they were able to get the others without anyone else getting hurt."

"You have to understand, I...I thought you were gone. You were pale, your lips turned blue, and I couldn't find a pulse. I thought you were dead, Georgia. Your blood was everywhere, pouring out on the floor and I couldn't stop it. So much blood and it was all my fault." He shuddered and closed his eyes, swallowing harshly. After a moment he continued. "I've seen brothers die, women and children slaughtered for no good reason. The ravages of war visited down on an unsuspecting populace. Never, have I ever felt as completely hopelessly lost as I did then." His hands shook as they continued to stroke her palm. "I couldn't live through that again. Losing you would be losing my soul."

His words fell upon her with the weight of an

elephant. She could hear the desperate plea in his voice, the unspoken request to never leave him. She knew the pain he felt was real for she felt it too. Losing him would be the same as finding a vital part of her existence suddenly gone.

"You didn't lose me, Levi. I'm right here."

"And I want you to stay here forever, in my life and my arms. I need you, Annabeth Switcher, and when you are feeling better, we're going to discuss this in more detail. I'm done with the long distance thing. After all that happened, I can't go back to how it was before. I love my SEAL brothers, but I'm going to ask for a transfer. Virginia Beach is still too far away, but at least it's not 2000 miles. We'll be able to see each other more often, and then, when it's time for me to re-enlist, I'm taking the option out. If we can hold it together for another sixteen months, I'll be yours full time."

The tears that filled Annabeth's eyes burned and caused his handsome face to blur. She squeezed his hand in hers. "No. You're not going to do that."

"Yes I am," he reiterated emphatically.

"No, you aren't because I'm moving to California. Just as soon as I can get out of this hospital and make the arrangements."

The choking sound coming from him frightened

her until she saw the look of awe on his face. "Honey, you have your career and your family on the east coast. I couldn't ask you..."

"You're not asking, I'm telling you. Besides, my job can be done anywhere. It's eighty percent electronic and telephone. Grace has her own life in Chattanooga. It's time for me to take my life by the horns and do what makes me happiest. That's you, Levi. You make me happiest. Everything else is just window dressing."

Hick stood so fast the recliner squealed on the linoleum floor. Leaning over the bed, he cupped her face in his hand and kissed her. He was warm and soft, gently brushing her plump lips with his. Instead of the passionate inferno that his kisses usually brought, this one was a slow smolder, full of promises and dreams of a lifetime together.

She slid her hand up, wrapping his hair around her fingers, holding on as he tenderly explored her mouth. He demanded nothing, but she yielded gratefully. She let his head go and looked up at him to see his eyes shiny and full of tears. Her big, beautiful, alpha SEAL was crying for her and the promise she had made to them both. Immediately, her cheeks dampened as tears rolled down them to disappear into her gown.

"Get some rest," he murmured to her then sat down in the chair. "We need you to get well so we can get this whole new life on the road."

"Sure thing, Hick," she whispered then closed her eyes. She was tired but so happy because now she knew she had made the right decision. When it came to her future, she knew Hick would always be the right decision.

CHAPTER 21

It had been six weeks since Phoenix. True to her word, Annabeth had made arrangements after being released from the hospital and promptly moved to California to be with him. Together, they had finished the little bungalow, and last week moved in together. He could never describe the joy at waking up with her in his arms every day.

Hick pushed thoughts of her to the back of his mind. Now was not the time to lose focus. The mission they were on was far too important.

"Eyes on Fedora; second floor, northeast corner."

Railroad's voice filled the earpiece. Hick's hands tightened on the assault rifle as he took several cleansing breaths. A deep sense of righteous satisfaction flooded him with the words. This time, al-

Bashir would not be getting away. One way or another, this all ended tonight. It was rather ironic that his greatest bid to hurt the United States had lead to this moment. It seems al-Bashir had sent one of his most trusted lieutenants to supervise the operation and had been caught sneaking over the Canadian border. It had taken time, but he had cracked. They now had more intel on the number one terrorist's activities than they ever had before including the location of his favorite safe house.

"Move into position," Bruiser murmured.

Cowboy, Finch, Abe, and Benny broke away, moving to the right until they disappeared on the left side of the wall. Likewise, Cookie, Wolf, and Toad moved to the right and faded into the darkness around the corner. That left Hick, Dude, Mozart, and Bruiser to take the main door opposite.

Once everyone was in place, the signal was given, and they all moved in.

The courtyard was quiet, and it took less than three seconds for Railroad to put the sentries down from his position on an outcropping rock overlooking the site. They had already dispatched the three men guarding the nest where Railroad now waited with his sniper rifle trained on the compound. As the last one crumpled to the hard packed sand, he affirmed the coast was clear.

Hick placed one hand on Bruiser's back as he felt Mozart do the same behind him. They would stay in constant contact once the lights were cut by Wolf's team. The twilight swallowed them as they advanced through the previously lit pools to the doorway looming in the distance. Quickly, Dude slapped charges to the hinge side of the door and motioned for everyone to move back. "Set," he murmured into his mic.

"Charges set," Cowboy whispered through the coms.

"Surveillance down," Toad confirmed.

"Everything's clear," Railroad replied.

"Go," Bruiser gave the command in a low monotone.

The silence of the compound was shattered as twin explosions ripped through the air and the compound was plunged into darkness. Hick flipped his tactical goggles down over his eyes. It took seconds for the eerie green glow to stabilize, and they were breaching the complex.

Moving as one, the unit poured into the house and spread out in the main living area. This looked more like what they had come to expect from the terrorist. Although everything was washed in the dull monotone green, they could tell it contained expensive furniture, wall hangings, and even tiled floors.

The area was in a state of chaos. Women screamed, and children cried as panic took them. A wide-eyed woman wearing traditional garb sprinted by them, but Dude grabbed her and pulled her kicking body against his. She began to stammer in her native language and pointing.

"The only word I can make out is 'baby,'" Hick's voice rose over the noise.

"Yeah, found them. We've got children," Abe's voice in their ears confirmed. "Six. Intel says there should be three more."

"We don't want this turning into a bloodbath," Wolf barked. "We have three minors somewhere in the building. Abe, you and Finch, stay with the kids. Dude, take her to them."

"Roger," the others answered.

A set of stairs materialized at the back of the large room. The thud of heavy footsteps echoed in the room as two men ran down, guns blazing in their hands. With two well-placed shots from Mozart and Hick, they fell and slid the final three steps. Hick grabbed one by the collar and pulled him out of the way. The rest of the team except for Abe and Finch assembled and quickly sprinted up the stairs and stepped out onto a landing. Another armed guard appeared and fired at them and was quickly dispatched.

Using hand signals, they split into two and took each side of the hallway. Systematically, they worked their way down the rows of rooms until only one was left. Hick knew from the sketched floor plan; this was Fedora's bedroom and office.

Wolf checked the knob and found the door locked. Hick slung his rifle to his back and dropped to his knees, pulling out a small kit from one of the pockets of his uniform. It took less than five seconds to pick the lock and return to his position behind the others.

With a kick of his booted foot, Wolf led the team into the room. They spread out along the wall as several voices screamed. Hick slapped the googles off his eyes as light flared to life on the other side of the room. Emergency lanterns bathed the area in a soft glow. What they saw made Hick want to curse.

Haafiz al-Bashir stood surrounded by several women and three children. He glared at the intruders as his black eyes danced maniacally in the flickering light. One of the women stood in front of him, his hand wrapped in her hair and her head pulled back. Her almond-shaped eyes were wide with terror as she glanced at the approaching men.

"Stop."

The words reached them easily. The man dubbed as Fedora by the task force and later identified as The Left Hand of Allah spat them at the intruders as he hid behind the woman. Quickly, he raised a wicked knife and pressed it against the woman's throat. A hiss rose from her lips as he nicked the surface and a drop of blood trickled down her dusky throat to saturate the translucent gown she wore.

"She's one of your wives. I don't think you want to hurt her." Wolf's tone was low and even from behind the sites of his assault rifle.

"She is but a woman - one that has disappointed and given me only worthless girl children. There are many more to replace her," he spat back angrily in his heavily accented tone. "I will have many more wives and many more sons. It is Allah's will."

"Can't father sons when you're dead," Wolf's reply was steady.

"Then I will have my seventy-two virgins and sit at Allah's side," he snapped. Quickly, before anyone could react, the knife plunged into the woman's throat, and he tossed her bleeding body aside. Screams filled the room as the other woman bolted with her hands covering her head. As she sprinted past, Benny snagged her and took her out of the room.

Grabbing one of the children, Fedora pulled her close to his body, wrapping an arm around her waist and lifting her until she covered his face. As before, the knife was pressed against her throat threateningly.

"Let the girl go."

"She is mine to do with as I wish."

Hick's memory of Annabeth being held in the same manner filled his mind. This man, hiding like a coward behind a twelve-year-old little girl was responsible for so many deaths. He was responsible for almost taking Annabeth from him. Hick's hand tightened on his rifle, causing the tactical gloves to squeak. There was no way in hell this bastard was getting away again.

"Last warning. Let. Her. Go." Wolf's voice was low and even.

"You will not risk harming her. "

Wolf grinned at him. "You'll be surprised what we'll risk."

The sound of suppressed fire reached them in

the room. Reflexively, Fedora turned his head, glancing at the window in the direction of the noise. When he did, the girl's body dropped a few inches, and his profile emerged over the top of her covered head. It was all they needed.

Gunfire filled the room along with the terrified screams of the children. Hick dropped his assault rifle, allowing it to swing from his shoulder by the strap. He caught the little girl that had fled towards him in his arms. She struggled, but he held her gently. Dropping to his knees, he murmured soft words to her, telling her she was safe, stroking her long dark hair tenderly. The child finally understood these men were not going to harm her and threw her arms around Hick's neck, burying her face against his chest as she cried and spoke in rapid Arabic. He didn't know what she was saying, but it didn't matter. Gently he lifted her in his arms and followed Cookie and Cowboy back down to the main room. Each was carrying one of the three girls. Wolf, Bruiser, and Toad remained in the bedroom, documenting the kill and taking DNA and photographic evidence.

Hick followed Dude as he led them back to the room containing the children. They were huddled in the center of the room around the two women sitting on the floor. Hick deposited the girl in the woman's arms and stepped back. Cookie and Cowboy handed off their charges as well.

None of the team had been hurt, and only one innocent had died. Hick's heart ached for the poor woman Fedora had killed, but that was on him. Hick liked to think it had been his bullet that had killed the bastard but they would never know for sure. The three holes in his skull were so closely grouped it there as no telling who had taken the kill shot. In the end, it didn't matter. The man responsible for so much death and destruction was gone. He thought seeing the mastermind behind the plan that had almost gotten Annabeth killed lying on the floor dead would be satisfying. Instead, he felt a sense of sadness for he knew that other monsters would surely rise to take his place. They had won this battle, but the war was far from over.

"Let's finish up and go home," Bruiser said as the lights were re-established in the building.

Hick couldn't have said it better.

CHAPTER 22

"Can I look now?"

Hick maneuvered Annabeth by holding on to her arms and gently pushing her forward. She had her hands out as she shuffled along.

"Not yet, beautiful. Almost."

He walked her over the sidewalk until they stopped before the cabin he had rented for them in the Colorado Mountains. Looking over her shoulder, he made sure the view was perfect then let out a held breath. He untied the scarf wrapped around her eyes and pulled it away. "Okay, look."

Annabeth's face lit up as she pressed her hands to her cheeks. He took a step to the side and watched the joy on her face as she discovered the special accommodations he had found for them. The cabin's sides were made of rough-hewn logs chinked with tan mortar with a wall of windows covering most of the front on the top story. A large porch wrapped around the front and disappeared around the back where a covered hot tub waited. The entire structure sat on a slight hill covered in leaves and pine needles. Her green eyes flicked over the cabin and zeroed in on the spectacular sea of yellows, red and oranges painting the mountains behind it. Her perfect lips circled in an 'O' of surprise. "Oh, Levi, it's beautiful!"

That was the reaction he was looking for. With a grin, he relaxed and tossed the scarf to rest on his shoulder. Taking her hand in his, he looked at the building through her eyes. The reality far exceeded the pictures sent to him by the booking agent.

"It's not bad. I was a little bummed when the original one I found wasn't available when we were ready. The agent suggested this one instead. It has a fireplace, hot tub, king size bed with down covers and vaulted ceilings. There's no sauna here, but I figured trading that for this view would be worth it. I hope you aren't too disappointed in having to wait two months past the time I promised you. On the bright side, we caught the September foliage perfectly."

She pulled her hand out of his and threw her arms around his neck. Looking him in the eyes, she smiled and shook her head gently. "I'm not disappointed at all. If you tell me the kitchen is full of food, so we don't have to leave this week, I'd call it perfect."

"I'll do you one better. I booked the concierge service to come here once a day. We'll have a nice meal daily." He nipped at her nose playfully. "We don't even have to get dressed if we don't want to. The chef will come, do his thing and leave without ever having to see us."

"I can't even begin to think how much this whole thing is costing you. It seems so extravagant."

He stared into her eyes, becoming lost in their liquid depths. Cupping her face tenderly, he whispered, "Nothing is too good for you, my Georgia. Every penny I spend on us is money well spent." He grinned at her mischievously. "Besides, how am I going to have my wicked way with you if I don't wine and dine you first?"

Her eyes sparkled with mirth as she took his teasing good-naturedly. "Those sound like pretty nefarious plans, Mr. Salter."

"Mmmhm. I have plans for you, Ms. Switcher. Wicked, sensual, naughty plans that will take the entire week to execute properly."

He saw the tiny hairs on her neck stand to attention at his words, and she shivered in his arms. Her eyes darkened with desire, and she licked her lips slowly causing a groan to erupt from him. She looked so damn delicious standing there in her jeans, sweater and those gawdawful ugly slouch boots she favored. Wisps of her crimson hair danced about her face as the chilled breeze caught them. Snagging one, he tucked it behind her ear then slid his hand to cup the nape of her neck. Staring deeply into her eyes, he traversed the slight distance between them and captured her lips in a tender kiss.

He tasted the sweet flavor of the strawberry balm she used as he nipped and sucked on her lips. A soft sigh brushed his mouth as she surrendered, pressing herself tightly against him. His hand slid up and under her sweater, splaying over her back in a possessive manner. She felt right in his arms, and he was never going to let her go. Slowly his hand slipped down, cupping her amazing rear in his palm and squeezing. She gasped and rubbed herself against him like a cat - all hot and feral.

The kiss deepened as the fire between them

leaped from smoldering embers to raging inferno. He felt her hands slip into the hair at the base of his neck, clutching desperately as she took his onslaught and returned it with renewed fever. Their tongues tangled and fought, stabbing impatiently as hands curled and nails scratched. He released her mouth, turning his attention to her jawline and neck, pressing hot kisses followed by nips and soothing licks until her breathing became pants and her legs trembled.

His eyes zeroed in on the silver line marring the creamy expanse of her shoulder. He had yet to forgive himself for her injury, but he knew she held no animosity toward him. Right then and there, he made a solemn oath to himself and her to never, ever allow her to be put into a situation where she could be harmed again. Yeah, part of him knew that was impossible, but at least the alpha male protector inside felt marginally better. When he remembered how close he had come to losing her, he felt sick. That was one feeling he never wanted to experience again.

He kissed the mark then followed it and bit playfully on the area where neck and shoulder met causing her to gasp and turn to goo in his arms. He grinned. He loved every squeak, moan and sigh from her.

"Hick?" Her voice had taken on that heavy drowsy sound he equated with her need for him. He forced himself to release her shoulder.

"Yeah?"

Her cheeks were flushed and her eyes bright. He felt her trembling against him as he held her tightly in his arms. She swallowed and bit her kiss-swollen lips. "I... I want you," she breathed.

He knew the smirk on his face would piss off most people, but not her. He pressed her tightly against him again, letting her feel the way she affected him. Nipping her ear, he whispered, "Then let's do something about that."

He reached down, hooking his hand under her knees and lifted her easily into his arms. She tightened hers around his neck and squealed as he picked her up. Carrying her onto the porch, he stopped at the door. "The keys are in my pocket."

She reached in, finding them easily then gave him a squeeze that made his eyes cross. "Naughty girl," he growled at her. She giggled, unlocked the door and opened it for him. He marched them across the hardwood floor, slammed the door with one foot then threw her on the oversized sofa facing a huge stone fireplace. "Too far to the bedroom," he answered her unasked question. Easing down on top of her, he slid his hand under her sweater and around to the back where he unfastened her bra. "You're not going to need that for a few days," he murmured then proceeded to undress her slowly. When she was bare, he took in her body appreciatively. "My beautiful Georgia. I love you more and more every single day, and I can't wait to show you how much."

"Then love me, Levi. Show me everything."

He smiled.

Later that evening, after they had finished the amazing dinner provided by the concierge service, Annabeth managed to get dressed despite Hick's best intentions. She had compromised and was wearing one of his Navy tee shirts and nothing else. It wasn't as loose as she would have liked, but it did at least cover her girl bits, so she wasn't flashing Bambi and the rest of the woodland creatures. It was silly to think that way, but she couldn't help herself.

All those gorgeous windows brought the outdoors right inside.

Standing at the sink, she dried the plates they had used and put them away. The cabin was beautiful and had all the amenities you could ask for. They had only been there one day, and already she was dreading having to leave. They had yet to try the hot tub, so she sent Hick out to make sure it was ready to go. After the workout they had in the bedroom, her sore muscles could use a nice long soak.

She heard her cell phone ding and frowned. Everyone knew she was going to be out of pocket this week and were told only call if it were a dire emergency. Dropping the dishtowel over the stove handle, she found her purse and dug in it until she found her cell. Pulling up her text messages, she saw it was from Hick. Most likely, he had gotten into the tub and was too lazy to get her, electing instead to send a message. She smiled to herself.

Swiping the screen, she looked at the emoji puzzle he had sent. They hadn't played the game much since Phoenix. First, she was recovering, then getting everything together to move and now living with him; it was just something they had let go. She wrinkled her brow as she studied the picture. It contained a man, a ring, a woman and a question mark. Normally, the answers came to her immediately, but this one was going to take a little time.

Keeping her eyes on the screen, she padded through the back to the deck. "I'm not sure I know this one. It may take me a..."

She looked up to see the man of her dreams on one knee. He had a dozen red roses cradled in one arm and the other lifted up towards her holding a small red velvet box containing a gorgeous ring with a beautiful emerald center surrounded by tiny diamonds.

The cell clattered to the floor as her eyes misted and her fingers covered her lips. She couldn't speak; only stare at him in shock as he grinned at her.

"Many years ago, my grandmother told me stories about how she and my grandfather had fallen in love on a ferry. They had a whirlwind romance that lasted less than a week before they were married. My grandfather worked hard to give her a life worth living. They started out with next to nothing, but he slaved away for years until he saved up enough money to open a small bistro in Boston. They worked together until it grew into three five star restaurants. On their fortieth anniversary, he gave her a beautiful pendant containing diamonds and emeralds, one for each of their three children and fourteen grandchildren. He told her family was their treasure. Three years later, he died of a heart attack while sitting at his desk. Grandmother had the pendant broken down into rings for each of us with the stipulation that we boys find the right one to give ours too. She said that we would be grafting into the family so to be careful of whom we choose."

He looked at the box in his hand. The emerald caught the light and reflected it back making it look as if a green fire burned in its center. "The minute I met you, I thought about this ring, waiting patiently in a lockbox. I fooled myself into believing it was just wishful thinking. We were friends, then friends with benefits and I told myself that is all we could be. But my heart knew better. For months, I wrestled with myself, going back and forth, trying to convince myself that we could only ever be friends. Each time I held you in my arms, I realized just how precious you were to me. Every time we parted, I felt a larger piece of my heart leave with you until there wasn't anything left of it with me. Annabeth, you are my heart. You are my life and my reason, and I can't imagine one more second of not having you be mine. I know we wanted to be casual and we've only recently moved into a personal, intimate relationship. I know we haven't discussed marriage, but I know you are it for me. I have made mistakes. I have hurt you, and I haven't always been there for you. But if you will let me, I'll spend every second of every day showing you how much I need and love you. Annabeth, will you let me love you? Will you let me care and cherish you until we are old and gray and die in each other's arms at 120 years old? Will you marry me?"

Annabeth's breath caught in her throat. Once upon a time, she had dreamed of the day she would be swept off her feet by a prince charming just like the books she devoured as a child. As she grew, she realized that not everyone had a happily ever after. But now? Now she could see it - a future with Hick, sharing that life worth living, holding on to each other through the bumps and pitfalls that awaited them. She smiled as tears slid down her cheeks and she nodded. Swallowing hard, she yelled, "Yes! Oh my God yes, Levi. I'll marry you."

He took the ring out of the box and placed it on her finger. Then rising, he drew her into his embrace and kissed her soundly. When he had finished, she looked at the ring. "Annabeth Salter. It has a nice sound to it."

He nuzzled her neck. "The best part? You won't have to change the monogram on your sheets."

"Speaking of sheets," her eyes found him, and she waggled her eyebrows suggestively.

"Yes ma'am," he intoned then swept her off her feet and took her into the bedroom.

EPILOGUE

The backyard of their little bungalow was full to bursting with friends, teammates and their women. Laughter filled the air as another glass was lifted in a toast.

"To Hick and Annabeth," Toad called out as he lifted his glass in the air. "May your lives be filled with love, happiness and lots of little arguments that become great makeup sex."

"To Hick and Annabeth," the others called out.

They downed their drinks and slammed their cups on the huge table taking up a large portion of the yard. Annabeth looked around at the magic that had been created there and felt her eyes mist over. She was so lucky to be a part of this amazing group.

They had gone all out to make their engagement party perfect.

"Those better not be tears of sorrow," Joselyn leaned over and whispered to her.

"They're not," she returned.

On the other side of her best friend, River sat with his arm around his wife's back, tenderly rubbing the large baby bump she sported as he talked with Abe. At almost seven months pregnant, she looked radiant even though she complained her ankles stayed swollen and the baby kicked incessantly. It was a beautiful sight, and it made the back of Annabeth throat tickle. This would be Joselyn's last trip before the baby came in December. She and River had flown out a few days ago to consult with the producer of the first Deidre movie. It was scheduled to be released at Christmas next year.

"How is the movie going?" Annabeth nudged her best friend.

"Amazing," Jos gushed. "I never knew that so much went into making a film. But if you want the real skinny, ask Demma. She is phenomenal as Deidre. They couldn't have picked a better actor."

Annabeth glanced down the table where the beautiful blonde starlet held court. She was surrounded by the wives of several SEALs, animatedly talking as her fiancé, Ryker McMillan watched on. Anyone could see the pride on Digger's face each time she leaned into him or touched his arm gently. They were so much in love; it was almost painful to watch.

"I plan on talking to her later if I can," Annabeth said.

"I think Alabama is a little star-struck. She told me she wanted an autograph but was afraid to ask for it. I'll put a bug in Dem's ear later to take a picture with her too." Joselyn chuckled softly. "I have a feeling social media feeds are going to blow up later tonight after everyone gets home. Between Demma and myself, I think we've taken a hundred photos."

"Ah, the life of a celebrity."

Joselyn chuckled.

"Annabeth. These clams are amazing! I've never had anything like this before. Who did you get to do the catering?" Bruiser leaned back and patted his stomach appreciatively.

"I didn't," she replied with a shrug. "Hick did it."

"The king of takeout," Railroad agreed. "He probably knows every hole in the wall dive for three counties."

"No, when I said Hick did it, I mean he *did* it. Everything you had tonight, he cooked."

The yard went silent as every person gawked at her. "No, seriously, where did he buy it? I bet it's that little seafood place down by the bay. You know, the one with all the antique fishing lures covering the walls," Cowboy told them. "Carls? Yeah, that's it. I bet it was Carls."

Hick chuckled softly and winked at Annabeth. "Told you," he said with a laugh. Picking up several of the plates, he took them into the house.

Annabeth glared at his teammates. "What is it with you bunch? He told me nobody would believe he cooked the meal. I don't know why you are all so shocked. Have I not been telling you bunch that he's an outstanding chef? I still don't see how it's possible that you guys don't like his cooking. After all, his family owns three five star restaurants in Boston. He even has a degree from Cambridge School of Culinary Arts!"

"Hick?" The look on the team's face was priceless.

Annabeth blew out a breath and nodded. "Yes, Hick."

Mozart looked down at the empty plate then at the shocked faces around him. "I thought you guys said never to let him cook for you? This was outstanding."

Bruiser rocketed to his feet. "Oh hell no. Hick get your ass out here. You have some 'splaining to do."

A moment later, Hick appeared at the door, carrying a large covered platter. Placing it on the table, he pulled the lid off.

"Jesus, is that tiramisu?" Finch craned his neck and gawked.

"Yep, from my grandfather's recipe."

"No, no, no. What is this? You feed us crap that would make a fly gag when we're in the field, but you have this whole hidden skill? What the hell, man?" Toad glared at him from across the table.

Hick's shoulders shook with laughter. "You guys remember how I got my rep, right?"

"Something about MRE's? Everyone was warned to not let you near anything edible. I heard one of your classmates ended up with food poisoning thanks to you." River was just as astounded as the others.

"I came in after this, but even I heard it," Railroad added.

"Tell it for the rest of us," Digger requested, "because something just isn't adding up."

Hick dropped into a chair next to Annabeth and

threw his arm around her shoulders. Instinctually, she snuggled against his side. He had told her all about his reputation with the team over his food while they had been at the cabin that week. Until then, she could never understand why they always gave him a hard time. "May as well start at the beginning," she murmured.

"Yeah, good idea. So, as Annabeth said, my family owns three places in Boston. The first one, *Genola's* was named after my Grandmother."

"Holy cow, I've heard of *Genola's*. It's won major awards for the cuisine," Benny said in amazement. "But, I thought Italian immigrants owned it. Forgive me for saying, but you look more like a California surfer."

"Yeah, I know," Hick agreed with a chuckle. Annabeth could see he loved every moment of this. "My mother is Louisa Bianchi-Salter. She met and fell in love with my father while on vacation in Hawaii. He's actually from Florida, but yeah, I took after him just like my brother. My sister, Antonia looks just like Mother with an olive complexion, dark eyes and a mass of pitch black hair. We are opposites."

He let that sink in a moment before continuing. "So, anyway, in typical Italian family way, I have a lot of cousins. All of us kids were raised in the kitchens. We were expected to take over someday after our parents got old and gray, so we were taught everything. I could make a Canadian maple Crème Brulee before I hit puberty." He motioned toward the untouched desert on the table. "That took a little longer. The recipe came over with Grandfather, and we weren't allowed to learn it until we were old enough to drive. Even then, it's committed to memory. We had to swear never to write it down."

As if reminded of its presence, everyone fell into the treat. Once plates were filled, and everyone settled down, he continued.

"Fast forward a few years. I started taking classes at Cambridge while still in high school and managed to finish the year after I graduated. Then, one day, I heard the news about that attack on the Little Rock recruiting center and something clicked. I enlisted the next day, much to my mother's dismay. Then Bud/s and here I am now."

"Okay, thanks for the history lesson," Toad grumbled between mouthfuls, "but get on with it. Get to the part where you decided to try and poison us in the field."

"It happened during a training mission right out of Bud/s. I hadn't been assigned a team yet, and we were all sitting around. Being raised as a foodie and always thinking about something different. I would experiment with the MREs. It became a game. I'd grab two of them out and mix the contents then try to figure out how to make it edible. One time I got this crazy chicken pot pie and tomato mixture thing. It was awful, but I was taught never to waste food, so I dug in any way. One of the others saw me eating it and asked for a bit. He wasn't impressed."

He chuckled at the memory. "Anyway, after that, a few other times one of the guys sampled my experiments, and I got the rep of not being able to cook. It didn't bother me because I knew better. By the time I got assigned to Bruise's team, my reputation had preceded me. I saw how when you guys were picking on me and my lack of culinary prowess, it took the edge off of the anxiety during fights. So, I figured I'd keep doing it. Its sort of had its own life since then. In my defense, I never did anything that would hurt anyone. I never gave anyone food poisoning - it was just an upset stomach and it was me not someone else. Anyway, I just carried the joke on each time. I always made sure to eat anything I created, even when I had to choke it down past my gag reflex a lot. You know, to keep me honest as it were." He shrugged. "And there you have it."

"No, un uh. Wait just a damned minute. You've been carrying on this joke for seven years?" Finch stared at him incredulously. "All this time, we've been trying to figure out ways to keep you from cooking, and you've been an ace in the hole the whole time?"

Hick grinned widely. "Yup."

"I'm sorry, Annabeth, but your fiancé is about to need traction." Cowboy pushed his sleeves up and stood up menacingly. "Do you know how much money I've spent over the last seven years to ensure someone else took your turn?"

"I do, and I thank you for your support."

They all stared at each other then the entire yard burst into laughter. "Oh man, that's a good one. But you realize now that we know you can cook, you're getting KP duty for like... forever." Bruiser wiped the tears of laughter from his eyes.

"No hardship there. It was harder to figure out new ways to ruin a meal than it would have to fix one."

Later that night, while everyone gathered around the open fireplace in the corner of the yard toasting marshmallows, Cowboy stood in the living room of Annabeth and Hick's newly refinished house and stared at his cell. When he had gotten the message a few moments ago, he had slipped off alone. The last thing he wanted was to dampen the festive spirit and his friend's engagement party. They had been through so much; they deserved some happiness. Now, in the privacy of this room, he could let the words from his sister, Marissa seep into his brain.

Father's taken a turn for the worse. The infection has spread, and he's been airlifted to the hospital. Please call me as soon as you can.

The call hadn't been pleasant. He knew that there had been complications after his father's surgery to remove his leg just above the knee. The doctor was sure they had gotten all of the cancerous growth, but his immune system had been ravaged by the cancer treatments until there was barely anything left. Within days of coming home, the stump had grown red and swollen netting him another trip in the hospital. In the three months since the surgery, he had spent almost half of it in and out of medical facilities. What was worse, the doctors didn't want to give him any more chemo or radiation until the infection was gone. They lived with the fear that cancer would return while he was too weak to fight it. Marissa got right to the point, telling him that the infection had gotten into his bones and they were going to have to take more of his leg as soon as he was strong enough for the surgery. They were currently dumping vast amounts of antibiotics into his system. Cowboy ended the call with a promise to come home as soon as he could. He could tell his sister was scared. He raked his hand through his hair. The alpha male protector in him was rearing his head.

"Shit," he swore softly. His fingers hovered over the keys, unsure what to say. Already, he had taken emergency leave when his father went through the surgery. He had just gotten back into the swing of things and now this. Mentally calculating, he knew he had at least twenty days leave accrued. It looked like he was going to have to take it. Before he told Marissa anything, he would have to talk to Bruiser and Commander Dixon. Typing out a quick email to ask for a meeting tomorrow at their earliest convenience, he sent it.

"Hey, Alcide, are you okay?"

Cowboy felt a heavy hand on his shoulder and

turned to see Digger standing there with worry on his face. "I saw you leave the party."

Shaking his head, he looked back at the cell then pocketed it. "Just some issues back home."

"Anything I can help with? You know my folks are just a few miles away from your family's spread. I know they would do anything they could."

Back in school, before he had decided to join the Navy, Cowboy had dated Digger's older cousin, Cindy. They hadn't run in the same circles, but Digger was from the same area as Cowboy. Familiarity bred comfort.

"Nah, I'm fine. So tell me, have you taken Demma home to meet the family yet?"

The puckered scar on the side of Digger's face pulled as a huge grin appeared. "Yeah, we went up a few weeks ago. We couldn't stay but a couple of days because they are still in production for the *Deidre Files* movie. My mom loves her, and my dad is completely enthralled. But then, that's my Demma. She manages to have everyone eating out of her hands and begging for seconds. I don't know what I ever did right to deserve that woman, but I thank my lucky stars I did. How about you? Is there anyone special on the horizon?"

Immediately, Cowboy's thoughts turned to Miley

Ellison, and the last time he had been home. Her grandfather, Doc Ellison, retired from veterinary medicine last year according to Cowboy's mother and left the practice to his granddaughter. They had butted heads a few times while he had been trying to get the ranch situated, but the sparks that flew between them were more than just their combined stubbornness. She stood all of five feet nothing and maybe weighted a buck five on a good day. With short chestnut hair she kept in a bob, large grey eyes, a turned up nose, and one of those Cupid's bow pouts, she had that cute pixie look that some men found appealing. Until the moment he set eyes on her, he wouldn't have thought he was one of them. His taste had always run in the tall, leggy blonde variety. It didn't matter anyway. Miley Ellison wouldn't even give him the time of day. She was all business and no play.

"Nah, I'm a perpetual bachelor." Draping his arm around Digger's shoulders, he walked toward the back door. "Come on; let's get back to the party. This is Hick and Annabeth's time. There will be time enough for me another day."

ABOUT THE AUTHOR

Melissa was born in Tupelo, Mississippi and raised in Houlka, a small rural town forty-five minutes southwest down the famous Natchez Trace. She found a love of reading very early and devoured everything she could. Told repeatedly that she had a wonderful imagination, she turned to scribbling her musings and wrote her first novel while in college. It was never published and has since vanished. The death of a close friend who aspired to become an author reawaked her own desire resulting in penning her first book, Shattered Dreams, published in 2013.

Melissa now resides in Meridian, Mississippi with her supportive family – husband, Robert and daughter Rebecca. When she isn't writing, she enjoys reading and talking with friends spread across the globe.

Website: https://www.mkclarke.com

Facebook: https://www.facebook.com/Melissakayclarke/

Twitter: https://twitter.com/MelissaKayClark

Blog: https://melissakayclarke.wordpress.com/

Instagram: @MKClarke

facebook.com/Melissakayclarke

amazon.com/Melissa-Kay-Clarke

ALSO BY MELISSA KAY CLARKE

Luna's Children

Shattered Dreams

Broken Melody

Lorestone: The Strength Within

The Legacy Reborn

Reclamation

Team Cerberus

Protecting Joselyn

Saving Olivia

Rescuing Annabeth

Safeguarding Miley

More Books in the Special Forces: Operation Alpha World!

Brynne Asher: Blackburn

Denise Agnew: Dangerous to Hold

Shauna Allen: Awakening Aubrey

Shauna Allen: Defending Danielle

Shauna Allen: Rescuing Rebekah

Shauna Allen: Saving Scarlett

Shauna Allen: Saving Grace

Jillian Anselmi: Protecting Ava

Jennifer Becker: Hiding Catherine

Julia Bright: Saving Lorelei

Victoria Bright: Surviving Savage

Victoria Bright: Going Ghost

Victoria Bright: Jostling Joker

Kendra Mei Chailyn: Beast

Kendra Mei Chailyn: Barbie

Kendra Mei Chailyn : Pitbull

Melissa Kay Clarke: Rescuing Annabeth

Samantha A. Cole: Handling Haven

Samantha A. Cole: Cheating the Devil

Sue Coletta: Hacked

Anne Conley: Redemption for Misty

Anne Conley: Mae Day

KaLyn Cooper: Rescuing Melina
Liz Crowe: Marking Mariah
Jordan Dane: Redemption for Avery
Jordan Dane: Fiona's Salvation
Delilah Devlin: Between a SEAL & A Hard Place
Delilah Devlin: Headover SEAL
Riley Edwards: Protecting Olivia
Riley Edwards: Redeeming Violet
Nicole Flockton: Protecting Maria
Nicole Flockton: Guarding Erin
Nicole Flockton: Guarding Suzie
Nicole Flockton: Guarding Brielle
Fifi Flowers: Protecting Maya
Fifi Flowers: Shielding Alice
Casey Hagen: Shielding Nebraska
Casey Hagen: Shielding Harlow
Desiree Holt: Protecting Maddie
Kathy Ivan: Saving Sarah
Kathy Ivan: Saving Savannah
Kathy Ivan: Saving Stephanie
Jesse Jacobson: Protecting Honor
Jesse Jacobson: Fighting for Honor
Jesse Jacobson: Defending Honor
Jesse Jacobson: Summer Breeze
Silver James: Rescue Moon
Silver James: SEAL Moon

Silver James: Assassin's Moon

Becca Jameson: Saving Sofia

Heather Long: Securing Arizona

Heather Long: Guarding Gertrude

Heather Long: Protecting Pilar

Kirsten Lynn: Joining Forces for Jesse

Margaret Madigan: Bang for the Buck

Margaret Madigan: Buck the System

Margaret Madigan: Jungle Buck

Margaret Madigan: December Chill

Rachel McNeely: The SEAL's Surprise Baby

Rachel McNeely: The SEAL's Surprise Bride

KD Michaels: Saving Laura

KD Michaels: Protecting Shane

Wren Michaels: Shadow of Doubt

Wren Michaels: The Fox & The Hound

Wren Michaels: Kisses from the Kremlin

Wren Michaels: Shadow of Doubt

Kat Mizera: Protecting Bobbi

LeTeisha Newton: Protecting Butterfly

LeTeisha Newton: Protecting Goddess

LeTeisha Newton: Protecting Vixen

LeTeisha Newton: Protecting Heartbeat

MJ Nightingale: Protecting Beauty

MJ Nightingale: Betting on Benny

MJ Nightingale: Protecting Secrets

Sarah O'Rourke: Saving Liberty

Debra Parmley: Protecting Pippa

Caleb Pirtle: Lovely Night to Die

Lainey Reese: Protecting New York

Jenika Snow: Protecting Lily

Jen Talty: Burning Desire

Jen Talty: Burning Kiss

Jen Talty: Burning Skies

Jen Talty: Burning Lies

Megan Vernon: Protecting Us

Megan Vernon: Protecting Earth

As you know, this book included at least one character from Susan Stoker's books. To check out more, see below.

Delta Force Heroes Series

Rescuing Rayne (FREE!)

Rescuing Aimee

Rescuing Emily

Rescuing Harley

Marrying Emily

Rescuing Kassie

Rescuing Bryn

Rescuing Casey

Rescuing Sadie

Rescuing Wendy

Rescuing Mary (Oct 2018)

Rescuing Macie (April 2019)

Badge of Honor: Texas Heroes Series

Justice for Mackenzie (FREE!)

Justice for Mickie

Justice for Corrie

Justice for Laine (novella)

Shelter for Elizabeth

Justice for Boone

Shelter for Adeline

Shelter for Sophie

Justice for Erin

Justice for Milena

Shelter for Blythe

Justice for Hope (Sept 2018)

Shelter for Quinn (Feb 2019)

Shelter for Koren (June 2019)

Shelter for Penelope (Oct 2019)

SEAL of Protection Series

Protecting Caroline (FREE!)

Protecting Alabama

Protecting Fiona

Marrying Caroline (novella)

Protecting Summer

Protecting Cheyenne

Protecting Jessyka

Protecting Julie (novella)

Protecting Melody

Protecting the Future

Protecting Alabama's Kids (novella)

Protecting Kiera (novella)

Protecting Dakota

SEAL of Protection: Legacy Series

Securing Caite (Jan 2019)

Securing Sidney (May 2019)

Securing Piper (Sept 2019)

Securing Zoey (TBA)

Securing Avery (TBA)

Securing Kalee (TBA)

New York Times, *USA Today* and *Wall Street Journal* Bestselling Author Susan Stoker has a heart as big as the state of Texas where she lives, but this all American girl has also spent the last fourteen years living in Missouri, California, Colorado, and Indiana. She's married to a retired Army man who now gets to follow *her* around the country.

She debuted her first series in 2014 and quickly followed that up with the SEAL of Protection Series, which solidified her love of writing and creating stories readers can get lost in.

If you enjoyed this book, or any book, please consider leaving a review. It's appreciated by authors more than you'll know.

www.stokeraces.com

susan@stokeraces.com

Made in the USA
Monee, IL
21 June 2020

34254405R00173